SMALLVILLE
**has suddenly become the scene of
the BIGGEST crisis on earth!**

Clark Kent's coming back to his hometown, Smallville, to attend his high school reunion, and to write a nice little feature story about it for *The Daily Planet*.

Superman is in town, too, to receive the mayor's commendation for a dramatic rescue mission. In fact, here comes the U.S. Army to add its special award to the honors being conferred. Only that's no general riding in the parade! That's no loving cup in the presentation box!

In full public view, Superman is about to receive a devastating blow from an adversary whose cunning may be a match for Superman's own incredible mind—a machine with no sense of right or wrong may, at last, destroy the greatest living force for good—Superman!

SUPERMAN III

A Novel by
William Kotzwinkle

Based on a Screenplay by
David Newman and
Leslie Newman

WARNER BOOKS

A Warner Communications Company

Warner Books, Inc.,
666 Fifth Avenue,
New York, N.Y. 10103

A Warner Communications Company

Printed in the United States of America

First Warner Printing: June, 1983

10 9 8 7 6 5 4 3 2 1

SUPERMAN III

PROLOGUE

Clark Kent made his way along through the streets of Metropolis as would any ordinary human being. When Clark was in his blue serge suit, behind his large thick glasses, he felt much as we all do, for he'd gotten accustomed to faking it. He faked it now, walking with measured timidity, a little jumpy, a trifle neurotic. Life on Earth was Clark's long mile...

"Excuse me...sorry..." Engrossed in thought, he'd stumbled against a woman in the street. She looked at him in disgust, for he'd upset her shopping bags, dislodging a pile of frozen dinners and sending them to the bottom of the bag on top of a pair of new designer jeans. "Watch where you're going, you four-eyed moron!" One hundred and fifty dollars for jeans, with frozen mashed potatoes in the pockets . . .

Thus, Clark Kent. Stumbling forward, a woman's withering stare on the back of his neck. Did she think he couldn't feel it starching his collar, making his uptight life even tighter? Would humanity never learn that accidents will happen?

And all along—I'm Superman.

All along, I carry for these people.

Tolerance, my son, came the voice of his departed father, speaking from an invisible dimension. *Bear with the Earth.*

Clark Kent continued along, as the inner voice faded. He would accept insults from strange women with shopping bags, and from Lois Lane. He was just Clark Kent the creep. Klutz and nebbish.

". . . pardon me . . . I'm terribly sorry . . ." Kent had just bumped into the one man in town blinder than himself, behind dark glasses.

The blind man turned with his seeing-eye dog; the dog eyed Kent suspiciously, but couldn't figure out his scent, some odd components in there somewhere . . .

The blind man tugged the dog back. Kent's clumsiness hadn't ruffled him; the dark was often rocky. "That's alright, buddy. But you ought to take it slower, y'know what I mean?"

"Yes sir, I do. And I think I need new glasses." Kent backed off apologetically, turned and bumped into a parking meter. But that happens to all of us from time to time, doesn't it?

The blind man continued on his rounds of downtown Metropolis, Monday morning, weather gray, outlook dark. His dog was thinking about the strange-smelling guy in blue serge, and sort-of nodded off, but the blind man was still angling into the street, confident his dog's head was screwed on straight.

"... that's it, boy ... take 'er through whatever's happenin' ..."

What was happening: A white-line pave-painter was rolling along down the street, with a rolling wheel full of paint, fast-drying. "... wonder if that paint's too thick ..." The painter kept checking the flow, for he did not want a slow-drying line. He did not see the seeing-eye dog, so intent was he on the quality of his paint in an effort to remain employed in an uncertain world. One mistake on a downtown line and he'd be painting highways in Hairshirt, Mississippi, with guys throwing muddy beer bottles at him.

"... good dog, good boy ..." said the blind man, flying on automatic in city traffic, on course with the line-painter, right angles.

Dog, daydreaming.

A collision is in the making, but there are other elements, for this is a street corner with hundreds of different trajectories, one of which belonged to a Miss Loreli Ambrosia, in whom wondrous body flow had been bestowed, enough to corkscrew the trajectory of an unemployed auto worker. Seeing Loreli, seeing her dress rolling like a sackful of puppies, he swiveled his head and walked backwards toward—

—the Penguin Salesman.

This gentleman had stolen his penguins only the night before, off a boxcar in a little-used siding by the river. They were perky little birds with plastic feathers and mechanical legs that walked them in circles on top of his table. "... alrigh' getchor penguins here..." He spoke as if people needed these penguins before getting on the subway, and perhaps they did. "... getchor little bird while it's on sale... inventory overload..." He wound a few more up, set them going. "... gettum while they're hot... take a bird to work..."

His eyes drooped, large bags under them, for night so often found the Penguin Salesman lugging stolen merchandise of little value through the streets of Metropolis. "... getchor birds right here... designer birds on sale..."

Loreli Ambrosia, something of a designer bird herself, stepped around a penguin, her hip jutting out. The Penguin Salesman lifted a drooping eyelid her way. "... how 'bout a bird, baby, got one you might like..."

The jobless auto worker, nerves destroyed by assembly lines, followed Loreli into the penguin table, upsetting them on the sidewalk. Twenty penguins walked off in different directions, some following Loreli, some following other desires.

The Penguin Salesman chased them wearily, so much of his life spent in situations like this. "... c'mere you little... getchor birds... pick yer fav'rite..." He banged full force into a little girl who was trying to cop one of his penguins; since she happened to be wearing roller skates she went flying backward, down the street.

She was on the way to ruining the breakfast of one Jimmy Olsen, photographer on the *Daily Planet,* who stepped up to his favorite hot dog wagon.

"Whaddya wan', mustahd, s'rkraud?" The Hot Dog Man stuck his fork indifferently into his mixtures, lifting, deploying, suggesting, wondering how many dogs he'd roll today, if he should buy crepe-soled shoes, would his mother-in-law move in on him. These thoughts proved idle, for in the next second his hot dog wagon sailed out from under his nose, its wheels set in motion by the roller-skating child who'd crashed into it.

Sauerkraut spritzed the air, and mustard flew, onto Jimmy Olsen, who was the sort of person life looks after that way. "...hey...hey...what about my hot dog..."

The Hot Dog Man was concerned for *all* his hot dogs, which were now leading an independent existence, wheeling on down the street, in a jet of steam. If the wagon dumped, he'd lose his buns. "...grab that wagon...someb'dy...grab...that..." His shoes were greasy and his runner's stride had never been perfected. His hot dog wagon gained on him. "...grab 'er...grab them ...dogs..."

No one was inclined to board the speeding wagon, what with sauerkraut dripping from it and mustard flying around. And yet, how far could a loose hot dog wagon expect to get in a city street? Ahead was a row of telephone booths, each booth occupied by your typical Metropolisian, oblivious to all but the instruments in their hands and the tiny voice at the other end. Imagine their surprise when they were run down by a hot dog wagon at nine-thirty, the booths tumbling like dominoes, occupants inside them. "... hey ... what the hell ... operator ... just a moment, operator, I've been struck by a hot dog wagon ..."

The last booth to fall contained a woman and her beloved poodle, who suddenly found himself being strangled on the end of a very tight leash. He coiled his neurotic little form and sprang free, trailing the leash down the street.

"... Sasha ... oh Sasha ... come back ..."

Sasha, unaccustomed to phone booths falling on him, yapped madly. His frenzied little bark drew the attention of the seeing-eye dog, and he, in a funk over Clark Kent's scent, bolted.

The blind man was left standing empty-handed in deep traffic.

The line-painter, only a few revolutions away, had the broken remnants of a hot dog wagon splintering around him, sauerkraut raining down on him and a poodle and a seeing-eye dog charging by.

He lost his grip on the wheel.

The blind man took it, in stride, and rolled the paint wheel on down the street. "... atta boy ... you sh'unt take off like that ... settle down now ..." Believing himself led by his dog once more, he painted one of the most confusing lines ever laid in downtown Metropolis, the sort of line only a windup penguin could follow.

"... getchor birds ... take two ... h'bout a nice bird fer yer ol' lady ..." The Penguin Salesman was retrieving his waddling stock, stuffing penguins in his pockets, but one of the faster models eluded him and waddled straight on, into a burning smudge pot at the edge of a construction site. The penguin caught fire and continued on.

Clark Kent wondered if he was seeing correctly. Was a small flaming bird approaching him? Had a Metropolis JD ignited a pigeon for laughs? Removing his horn-rims he gave the spectacle a penetrating glance.

"... hmmmmmn ... a burning penguin ..."

Kent went into action, like the good civilian he was, and blew out the burning penguin.

"... alrigh' buddy, it's yours ..." The Penguin Salesman was right beside him. "... it's a little scorched, I'm havin' a fire sale ... you get it for two bits ..."

"Oh...yes, yes of course..." Clark Kent forked over the money and continued along with his burnt bird. *Taken again,* he reflected, as we all so often do in great Metropolis.

A bank guard down the street was at that moment having that very reflection as his arms were twisted into the pinned position behind him and a second robber walked on through the front door. The guard shook his head to himself, for he would be in trouble over this, especially if anybody got themselves shot in the process, especially himself.

"...take it easy, pal, I've got rheumatism in that arm...I usta pitch for the Mets..."

"So don't move," growled the bandit behind him.

"I ain't movin'. I may look like I'm movin' but I ain't..."

Where is Superman? Isn't this his kind of moment?

He is contemplating a charred plastic penguin.

So the prayer of one bank director with a gun at his head is directed elsewhere. "Don't shoot me, mister, particularly not in the head."

"Open the vault."

"It's open, it's yours, take it right off the hinges."

A bank vault is a cozy place, the money sleeping there, some of it in silver, some in gold, a nice sackful. The robber filled the sack quickly, his heart in overdrive, his fingers flying at the biggest haul he'd ever made. Please, god, get me outa here fast with both hands full...

The bank guard was practicing an advanced yoga posture, elbows touching the hard way, folded in back like chicken wings. "Make one move an' I'll snap them up to your *ears*."

"I'm froze, buddy...like a plastic turd, ok? Don't break no bones, I gotta pitch t'morra." The guard stared toward the bank vault, from which the other robber was racing, a sack over his shoulder. The guard went flying face forward, his captor propelling him off balance toward the floor. He rolled left, in a quick feint, then, hearing no gunfire he rose. The bank was already empty. He blew his whistle, stuck a finger in the air, and wondered if there were any other preparatory moves he could possibly make.

The robbers diverged toward their car, the one with the sack going around back, legs flying. He'd made a big score at last! He'd grabbed enough swag to start his own video arcade in a nice small town somewhere...

His triumphant dream was marred by hideous coincidence. Directly behind him a workman was removing a ladder from his van. Unaware of the dramatic events transpiring, the workman rotated in easy fashion with his ladder, its claw hooks snagging the sackful of loot, wrenching it from the robber's hands.

"You sonofa—"

"What'd I do to you?" The workman stared at the armed robber. The robber leapt for the money dangling at the end of the ladder. Something like this happened on every job, something out of the blue, one time it was a monster flock of robins in the road, and now this...goddamned...ladder...

He reached for his fortune, just as Fortune herself reached for it, in the form of a large construction crane, of the kind called a cherry picker. It picked the bag off the ladder and swung it upward.

"...that's it...I'm through with this racket..." The robber turned, leapt in the getaway car screeching by him. His partner looked at him. "Where's the dough?"

"On the roof," sighed the robber and slouched

into his seat. On top of everything else the bank guard was out now, crouching on the sidewalk, gun raised. It was one of those days, probably the full moon or something, when everything you try goes wrong.

"Fire, Officer O'Houlihan!" cried the bank director.

"Yessir," said O'Houlihan, though he didn't want to rush the shot. He wanted to take careful aim, bring the vehicle to a halt, and see his picture in the *Daily Planet*. He tracked carefully, and squeezed the trigger.

A cabbie screeched into the firing line, and bought Officer O'Houlihan's bullet in the bumper, with a ricochet into the front tire. The cabbie fought the wheel, but his velocity, like that of all cabbies, was too great. He sailed on by his fare, and found himself skidding toward the curb. "...hunk of junk they give you to ride aroun' in..."

Collision with a fire hydrant gave him something to think about, as the hydrant exploded in a gusher of water that started to fill his cab. He yanked at the door, but as usual it was stuck. "...hackin'...I've been hackin' long enough..." He frantically grabbed the window handle, which came off in his fist. "...drown in this sumbitch..." He crawled past his meter, with water rising around him. The flag on the meter popped up momentarily and then submerged. The cabbie grabbed his CB mike. "...gimme the Dispatcher..." The water came up, around his neck. "...I'm drownin'...over on Forty-seventh . . . musta drove in a fountain, I dunno . . . can you send the wrecker?''

He lost the mike in the boiling turmoil of the water and then went down, into the waves.

Clark Kent, observing a man drowning in his own car, went directly into action. He turned in the opposite direction, toward a phone booth, wherein he would change out of his blue serge into the uniform of power and courage. Unfortunately, the phone booths had all been flattened by the runaway hot dog wagon, so he was forced to leap into a Photomat Booth. There a profound transformation took place.

He was photographed four times, in four stages of undress, culminating as SUPERMAN! These revealing photos spit out of a slot in the machine, where they were immediately grabbed by a perverted child, the sort who can't walk by a Photomat Booth without being aroused. Eagerly he started to look at the telltale photos, but they were ripped from his hand. Superman tore off the top three, of Clark in his underwear, and left the child with but one of the photos, to inspire him all his life, a photo of SUPERMAN!

Then he flew off down the street.

The cabbie was going under for the third time, weighed by twelve hours' worth of fares in his change purse. He slumped under the dashboard, into the depths, arms flailing helplessly. *Drowned . . . in my own . . . cab . . .*

Superman knocked on the window to reassure him. The cabbie made feeble swimming gestures.

17

Superman tore the roof off the car and extracted the drowning man. He laid him on the sidewalk and then turned toward the flooded cab.

". . . leave it . . ." The soggy cabbie staggered to his feet. ". . . the balljoints are gone . . ."

Superman, however, had to contend with the gushing hydrant. He lifted the ruined taxi from it, then jammed the broken hydrant back into the ground like a cork in a bottle.

"Way to go, Superman!" yelled young Jimmy Olsen of the *Daily Planet,* mustard still on his face and sauerkraut in his hair, thereby increasing his already close resemblance to a hot dog.

"Hi, Jimmy," said Superman, "how are you?" The greatest of men prepared to return to the Photomat Booth, change, retrieve his burnt penguin, and continue on to work. Yet something inside him said, wait, you'll only have to change back again in about ten seconds.

What's going on? wondered Superman. I can feel something . . .

He quickly scanned the street, up and down, and then across, to the vest-pocket park for children which the city had thoughtfully placed in its midst, so that laughing innocent voices might remind us to smile all day long, though at night it was worth your life to go there. At this moment, however, a babbling nanny was placing her toddler on the end of a seesaw. "There, sweet little Nathaniel. And now I'll get on the other end and give you a lovely ride."

Still babbling, she walked around the seesaw to

the other side and prepared to place her leg up over the seat. High above this simple soul, the cherry picker crane had deposited the sack of money on an adjacent roof. There it had lain beside a crew of thirty-story riveters and welders. "... you see Reggie cum to the plate las' night? One pitch an *boom-bah* ..."

"Yeah, he really burnt out their nose hairs. Hand me that bag of rivets ... no, not those, that other bag ..."

"... heavy sucker, ain't it? Who loaded this thing, King Kong?"

"Hey, watch where yer goin' ..."

"You tellin' me how to ... how to ... whooooo-aaa ..."

"WATCH OUT BELOW!"

The sack of precious metal was now hurtling downward, its shape a blur. Directly in line with its bulging bottom was the nanny, still trying to get her corrective stocking up over the edge of the seesaw. Her life itself may have been saved by the difficulty of this maneuver. "... soon, Nathaniel, we'll be going gently ... up and down ..."

The sack hit the seesaw squarely, driving the end down and sending little Nathaniel up like a rocket in the air. The toddler dribbled ecstatically; he'd never expected they'd get down to some real playing, but this—sailing straight up in the air— was al-*right*.

Children don't worry about coming down. If chance catapults them hundreds of feet in the air, that's fine. And so, little Nathaniel reached the zenith of his arc, burped, and smiled. Then suddenly he was dropping, his shape a blur seen by none but—SUPERMAN!

The Man of Steel rescued the toddler, naturally, but his flying form startled a pair of sign painters working on the side of a building. "Mike, look who's here!"

"Hey, Superman, how's it goin'..."

The jet stream of his passing figure spun one of the sign painters around on his scaffold, so that he ended up clutching his ropes, and dangling. "...don't...rock..." he whispered to his partner. "Whatever you do...don't rock..."

"I ain't rockin'...come on...crawl slow...take holt of my wrist."

The dangling sign painter crawled slowly toward his partner. "...bastid flyin' by like that..."

"Hey, he was savin' a baby."

"...an' I'm out here hangin' by my jockstrap..."

"It's ok now...come on...that's it."

The sign painter regained his balance at the far end of the scaffold, brushed himself off, adjusted his overall straps. "Fourteen years that's the closest I've come."

"Yer alright now."

Neither man saw that in their struggle on the scaffold, one of their paint cans had walked to the edge. An unhappy paint can, it decided to jump; a few drops of paint spilled from its lip as it wobbled back and forth.

"...hmmmmmn...looks like rain..." Far below, a gentleman tentatively opened his umbrella;

feeling no further precipitation, however, he closed the umbrella. Then the gallon of paint landed on his head.

This remarkable chain of events might have ended here; but the momentum was not yet spent, for a man with a can of paint on his head is liable to do anything. After flailing about in crazed fashion, he finally succeeded in knocking over a gumball machine; little personal comfort was derived from this but a considerable number of gumballs did go rolling down the sidewalk.

Rolling gumballs are hazardous, as we all know.

". . . and now, ladies and gentlemen, I'd like to present my colleague, the lovable street mime, Jo-Jo the Silent One . . ."

Patrons of a nearby sidewalk café, many against their will, were now gazing at the mimicry of Jo-Jo, cheeks painted, pants bagging, a self-satisfied smirk on his face as he faced the sidewalk tables.

There are many sights one might request while waiting for one's morning coffee, but Jo-Jo the lovable mime pretending to climb a hill in a windstorm probably isn't one of them. Newspapers rattled, teaspoons clicked nervously; one hungover patron put his head in his hands and prayed for the Sanitation Department to come along. But lovable Jo-Jo continued his brilliant performance, hat flying, arms waving in quick staccato movements of the sort that cause headaches if watched at breakfast. So engrossed was he in the fine points of his technique that he didn't see the rolling gumballs until they were under his feet.

". . . what the helllllll . . ." Jo-Jo the Silent One spoke, as he lost his balance, wheeled upside down, and fell on his elbows.

"Hey, that's pretty good."

". . . yeah, let's see that one again, Jo-Jo . . ."

Impelled along their way by Jo-Jo's flying feet, the gumballs continued down the street in loose formation. Anyone familiar with the habits of rolling gumballs knows they are unlikely to stop until they find a delivery man carrying a tray of custard pies.

". . . had a helluva night last night, some nut drillin' through my ceiling . . ."

"No kiddin'? How many of these custard you wan'?"

"Lemme have a dozen."

This conversation, between a tired delivery man and a baker's helper, was taking place in a building just ahead of the rolling gumballs. The delivery man lifted the tray of twelve custard pies, and walked into the street; he might've sidestepped the gumballs but, as mentioned, a nut had been drilling through his ceiling the night before and he was not himself this morning. He stepped on a gumball and his pies went flying.

A flying pie is a beautiful thing.

Loreli Ambrosia is also a beautiful thing, with a fresh, natural, down-to-earth beauty, simple and uncomplicated. Imagine her horror when she saw a custard pie sailing wildly through the air. *Hours I spent on this makeup job,* she remarked to herself as the pie sped toward her. *If custard gets in these false eyelashes my head will fall off.*

A deft hand reached out beside her, blue serge flashing. It was Clark Kent, always the perfect gentleman, ever ready to protect a young lady from getting pie on her blusher. So swiftly did his hand move, so quickly did he whip the pie away that Loreli now believed it to have been just a momentary illusion, for where was the pie now?

It was in the face of the man standing behind Clark Kent.

"...*whubbb*...*hobbend*...?" The man desperately tore at the custard, thinking he'd fallen into a vat.

"Oh," said Kent. "Sorry about that."

"...*sorrbee? You smunnnamabish*..." The man tried to fling custard at Kent, but Kent had moved on to the corner, where he now waited for the light to change.

Terribly clumsy of me to put a pie in that man's face.

Clark reflected in quiet sobriety, as the light changed to amber.

Think how he must feel, custard up his nostril.

The amber flickered. Clark prepared to step from the curb. A truck, at the same time, sped up to beat the light. The driver's view was partially obstructed owing to his left eye having been punched closed by his wife at breakfast. He barreled through a mud puddle, causing it to spray all over Clark Kent, whom he now saw, standing drenched. "Sorry, pal," said the trucker, but in such a way, with such a sneering grin that Clark knew he wasn't really sorry.

If you were the mightiest man on Earth, and an ignorant boor had just splashed water all over you, wouldn't you feel like teaching him some manners? Put his cigar out in his ear, for example? Tear his *Drink Beer* T-shirt to shreds?

These things occurred to Kent. But he repressed his anger, which as we know isn't healthy.

All that repression is going to catch up to you, Clark.

How long can you go on eating humble pie?

One day you're going to explode . . . .

1

In the heart of downtown Metropolis, a man was playing with his yo-yo, the scarred wooden wheel spinning above the floor of the Unemployment Office. He checked out movement down the line, and went on spinning.

"What's happenin', brother." A fellow recipient of some much-needed government attention stood on the next line, rearranging the holes in his pants pockets. The man with the yo-yo turned and flicked out a fast orbit of the spinning wheel. "Goin' round and round," he said, a single gold tooth flashing in the midst of his brilliant smile, heightened by the dark walnut of his skin. He stepped forward in line, for the thirty-sixth week in succession. Close observers of yo-yo technique will note a slight wobble in his spin, something that happens to all unemployment recipients on week thirty-six.

Too soon, the clerk beyond the counter was staring into his eyes. She had heard thousands of stories, twisted in every possible direction, and her ears were now stone, to match her heart. "Name?"

"Gus Gorman." The yo-yo whizzed down in a silent walk-the-doggie, beyond the woman's view. Gus watched as she pulled out his folder. A scowl was starting to cross her face, as if she were discovering a plot to kidnap her children. "Have you looked for work this week, Mr. Gorman?"

"Been lookin' night and day." Gus's yo-yo snapped behind his back in a crossways pendulum, whirring softly beneath the sounds of the big office and skimming by his worn-down shoe heels.

"For what kind of work?"

"Kitchen technician."

"Dishwasher." The clerk shuffled the file. "Mr. Gorman, according to our records you have been unemployed for thirty-six weeks."

"Thirty-five ..."

"You secured employment last June as a messenger and were discharged after one day." She looked up at him, her eyebrow lifting slowly; the plot to kidnap her children had now been matched by one to poison her dog and beat her tulips with a hammer. "Well?"

"They said I lost it on the subway, but it's not true." Gus's yo-yo snapped into his palm. "A pickpocket took it."

"A *television set?*"

Gus smiled innocently. He'd sold the TV set to a needy family. You find those kinds of opportunities every now and then, and Gus always took advantage of them.

The clerk lowered her eyes to the file again, which, to judge by her expression, had turned into a piece of parchment made from human flesh by the man standing before her. "The only other employment you found was in a fast-food chain. Employment lasted twenty-eight minutes." She looked up. "I believe that's a record with this office."

Gus's yo-yo buzzed over his shoe tips, a tiny polishing cloth attached to heighten the shine. His mind had been occupied at the fast-food chain; he had higher things to think about than hold-the-pickle and extra-onions. He'd been seeing the Yo-Yo of yo-yos in his dreams, string shining in the most complicated pattern he'd ever seen. A man cannot deal french fries at such a moment of inspiration.

"Mr. Gorman—" The clerk was tapping the edge of the file folder. "—you have spent thirty-six weeks living off the taxes of hardworking citizens." A sensual quiver flared her nostrils. "Do you know what you are?"

"Don't call me a bum. Don't say it."

Her lips parted moistly. "You are no longer eligible."

The man beside Gus said in a soft voice, "She gets off on that line, don't she . . ."

Gus turned with his yo-yo, leaving the records and files behind him, none of it important now, and the whole building no longer part of his scene. The moment had a feeling of freedom to it, which would last until lunchtime, when the feeling of hunger would replace it. He walked to the exit, where he took a crumpled pack of cigarettes from his pocket, extracting the last wrinkled cigarette. He put it to his lips, but lacked a match. Here Fate, in the form of an unemployed elevator operator, intervened. The operator, telling some pals about life in the shaft, saw Gus fumbling for a light and slipped him a match flap, then returned to his narration: "... in the cellar of the place, I'd open the elevator door and giant *rats* would be there, waiting to get on. I *had* to quit that job..."

The tale, like so many epic narratives heard in unemployment office hallways, had to fade half finished, as Gus descended the stairs. He tore the last match from the flap and was about to glide the flap into a trash can, when the ad printed on the cover caught his eye.

His mental yo-yo came on, the string buzzing in his brain and describing a circuitry so complicated and yet so smoothly functioning that Gus continued to stare at the ad; thousands of mind-strings flashed in his head, yo-yos flying in every direction in a beautifully controlled performance.

EARN BIG MONEY
BECOME A COMPUTER PROGRAMMER

Gus folded the flap gently in his fingers and slipped it into his pocket. "Gonna have to look into this," he said, for when the Big Yo-Yo spoke, a man would be a fool not to listen.

". . . as Chief Instructor of the Archibald Data Processing School, it is my honor to introduce you to Henry, our machine. Henry, say hello."

The instructor typed on the computer keyboard, and the screen flashed a greeting. *"Hello, class..."*

Far far out, thought Gus Gorman to himself.

Gus had been in typing class once, long ago. He'd been cool with it too; when the teacher said *go* in the test, Gus was already halfway down the page . . .

". . . computers as we know . . . capable of quite remarkable activities, chief among them the function of . . ."

The instructor pressed a button:

". . . *memory* . . ." said Henry the Computer. *"I am a function of . . ."*

Memory, thought Gus.

He had the whole thing in his mind somewhere, up there with his yo-yo strings.

His wrist flipped out, an under-the-kneecap move, yo-yo suspended momentarily in the air.

I know something 'bout this already . . .

Gus had built short-wave radios as a boy to monitor police progress in the neighborhood; when his uncle brought home a stolen adding machine, Gus'd taken it completely apart and put it back together again; when his father threw a saxophone through the TV screen, he'd been able to replace the tubes; then he'd wired his own snooping device and lowered it into the bedroom of the call girl living below, which brought him to the attention of her boyfriend, a local gangland kingpin who gave him work as a wiretapper. Gus might have made a career of this, but after his employer was thrown off a building, Gus drifted out of electronics. His natural engineering ability faded into the background, except for an astonishing skill with video games, whose devious pathways seemed obvious to him; his Pac-Man scores were phenomenal but of little social value. Kitchen technician had become his career—until now—

—because this computer he was looking at was first cousin to Pac-Man and second cousin to a pinball machine.

". . . in which we have strings of data . . ."

Strings, thought Gus, looking down at his yo-yo. Always knew this instrument was tryin' to tell me something.

". . . string variables are labeled with a dollar sign . . ."

Make perfect sense, thought Gus.

". . . what we call *looping it* . . ."

Gus looped his yo-yo round and round. Yessir, it's all clear as a goddamn bell . . .

The instructor smiled at his class, as lights went beeping by, the greater glory of Archibald Data Processing School, alma mater of few, two flights up, above a grocery store.

". . . notice the floating decimal point . . ."

". . . see it clearly," said Gus, scanning with the man.

* * *

Elsewhere in Metropolis, in the offices of the *Daily Planet*, another skull conference was going on, directed by Perry White, editor of the Planet, a hard-headed guy with much understanding of the world and little knowledge of people like Clark Kent. Or of Jimmy Olsen who, looking like a hot dog, stood beside Perry White now.

"Who's this?" snarled White, pointing at a glossy news photo Olsen had taken and developed himself, with great pains and sauerkraut on his sleeve.

"That's Ross Webster, sir. Winner of the Humanitarian of the Year award. I gave him f.two at a fiftieth."

White chomped on his cigar, his lower lip in a cynical sneer. "Olsen, somebody oughta give you f.two in the mouth. If this guy is the Humanitarian of the Year, why do I have only one picture of *him* and fifteen pictures of *this* person?" Perry White stabbed his cigar tip at a spreading fan of glamor shots.

"That's Loreli Ambrosia. She's Webster's..., ah...she's Webster's..."

"She's Webster's," interrupted Lois Lane. "Let's just leave it at that."

Jimmy Olsen removed the sauerkraut from his sleeve and pointed at Webster again. "He owns Webcoe Industries." Olsen, not knowing he also had mustard on his nose, flashed another picture down for White's perusal. "This is his sister."

"A hard-looking broad," said White. He lifted

the picture up and examined it more closely. "It's out of focus, you nitwit."

"There's something blurry about the woman, Mr. White." Olsen fumbled. "Some kind of natural veil around her."

"There's some kind of natural veil around you, Olsen. Did you walk through a wall of flaming vaseline?"

"Excuse me, sir?"

"Don't interrupt—" White was chewing his cigar, staring at Vera Webster, sister of Ross Webster. "This woman is a trained spinster." He tapped the photo with his finger. "Am I right, Lois?"

"Right, Chief."

Perry White shifted his cigar to the other corner of his mouth. "She looks like she could freeze a monkey's—"

The door opened and Miss Henderson from Circulation entered. She could also freeze monkeys, if she had to. She was grumpy, middle-aged, and pushing a Bingo machine, which quite possibly made her feel grumpy, for it was heavy and filled with white plastic balls. Perry White turned on her.

"Whaddya want?"

"It's time," said Miss Henderson, "for you to draw this month's winning Jingo number."

"Why should I?" growled Perry White, but Miss Henderson was already pushing the Bingo Jingo machine under his cigar. She turned toward Lois Lane. "First prize is an all-expenses-paid trip to South America." Miss Henderson performed a rumba step of the most outlandish kind.

"Settle down, Miss Henderson," said White. He took unwilling hold of the crank of the large transparent Bingo barrel. "Why can't they get the idiot in Circulation who dreamed up this imbecilic contest—"

"Let me get a shot of it, Chief," said Olsen. "I'll give you f.two too."

"Ftwo you, Olsen," said White, smoke billowing around him as he started to crank the handle.

"It'll never replace the printing press, Chief," quipped Lois Lane.

White spun the handle faster, and set the white balls bouncing inside the barrel. They clicked and tumbled merrily around, and he became fascinated, twirling the crank faster.

"Excuse me, Mr. White," said Clark Kent, entering the office.

"Not now, Kent, I'm trying to put out a newspaper here." White studied the bouncing balls, wondering if he could possibly keep them all in the air at one time, or blend them at the center somehow . . .

Clark Kent turned to Jimmy Olsen. "You have mustard on your nose."

"Smile, Mr. White."

"I never smile, Olsen, it's bad for my image."

"Hi, Lois," said Clark Kent, adjusting his glasses and smiling at the warped image of Lois beyond them.

"Hi, Clark," she said indifferently, finding plastic balls more interesting. "What's the winning number, Chief?"

"How the hell should I know?" White slowed the machine as one tumbled out. He picked up the little egg-shaped object and pried it open. "Fifty-three."

"Fifty-three!" shrieked Miss Henderson toward the Circulation department, her neck stretching out like a bolting ostrich.

"Control yourself, Miss Henderson." White pushed the Bingo Jingo machine back toward her. "And take this out of here."

Miss Henderson's eyebrow shot up in chiseled resolve. "You've got to pick three more numbers."

"Oh, for god's sake." White resumed cranking.

"Looks great, Chief," said Jimmy Olsen. "I'm giving you—"

"Shut up, Olsen."

"Yessir."

Clark Kent stepped forward. He and Perry White had been discussing a story idea last night when the paper went to bed and Clark was still hot for it, naive fool that he was. "Mr. White, about that story we discussed—"

"I don't know yet, Kent . . ."

"Personally, sir, I think it would be a terrific story," said Clark, in his boyish fashion.

"*What* terrific story?" asked Lois Lane, worried that Clark might be scooping her on something. Like all newswomen she had the veneer of a mass-produced coffee table, and did not like anybody getting ahead of her.

White looked up from cranking his machine, and gave Lois his don't-worry-about-the-boy-scout look. "Kent's been invited to his high school class reunion." He looked at Kent. "So who cares?"

"Going to your high school reunion is practically a ritual in America," said Kent. He turned to Olsen for support. "Isn't that right, Jimmy?"

"I wouldn't know, Mr. Kent. Most of the people I went to high school with are still in high school."

Miss Henderson cranked her head around toward White, putting her grump's face in front of his. "*Could* we have the next number?"

Perry White spun the barrel again, and reached into the slot. "Here's your plastic egg, Miss Henderson, go hatch it."

"Thirty-three!" shrieked Miss Henderson on tiptoe toward Circulation.

"She's all chicken," said White, admiringly, and continued cranking the handle, as Clark Kent pushed his argument forward once more, a crushed gumball adhering to the bottom of his shoe.

"What the story is really about is how the typical small town has changed in the last fifteen years. Take me, for instance—"

"I do take you, Kent. Every day. Like medicine." White cranked angrily on, Miss Henderson bearing down on him, and Clark Kent yammering about his high school.

"Can I really go back to middle America," asked Kent, "after having become a Metropolis sophisticate?"

He looked meaningfully at Lois. She looked back at him, wondering in what way he thought he was sophisticated. His glasses looked like he'd bought them at Woolworth's and the cut of his suit was early Salvation Army. She spoke none of this, not wishing to hurt the poor boob's feelings.

Clark whipped his briefcase forward, banging his own kneecap, and snapped it open. Tucked within the briefcase was a folded maroon garment. "I was looking through my closet last night and I found my old high school sweater." He unfolded it and held it proudly in front of him. Sewn in the middle of the chest was a big white block letter S.

"Superman?" asked Lois Lane, faint mockery in her voice.

"Smallville," said Kent, and thought back nostalgically to his high school days for a moment, during which he'd been continually humiliated.

"I'm getting a cramp in my elbow," said Perry White.

"*Mr.* White," said Miss Henderson, face puckering. "May we *please* have the next number for Circulation?"

"How's *your* circulation, Miss Henderson," said White with a cruel laugh. "This machine might improve it."

"That's not funny, Mr. White," said Miss Henderson, whose feet were notoriously cold, especially at night.

"Let me crank that for you, Mr. White," said Clark Kent, stepping up to the machine. He gripped its handle with his great Kryptonic strength, and set the barrel tumbling. "So, Mr. White? Can I go ahead with my travel arrangements?"

Lois Lane stepped between them. "Perry, I'd like to make some travel arrangements of my own." Her elbow touched Clark's, causing his joint to spin excitedly. The crank handle whirled as his arm went up and down; the handle came off in his hand. He stared at it; one Bingo Jingo handle, rendered useless by his clumsiness.

Why, wondered Clark Kent, am I such a klutz? After all, I'm SUPERMAN!

And yet, when I get in this blue serge suit and put on these glasses, I truly seem to lose my mind.

He longed to pop out of his three-piece and into his acrobat uniform and crank the heavens with his handle, the handle of SUPERMAN!

But that would be immodest. No, I must stand here with everyone laughing at me as I hold this crank in my hand, my mind going like lightning, reading every nuance of Perry White's mockery.

"I always knew you were a crank, Kent," said White, chuckling to himself. He turned to Miss Henderson. "Alright, get this Jingo machine out of my office."

"Mr. White, you *still* have one more number to draw," said Miss Henderson, and pointed at the drum, her finger stiff as a popsicle stick.

"Alright, alright..." White knew he'd have no peace until he got this Jingo-crazed woman off his back. "Put that crank back on, Kent."

"I can't, sir. It's—cracked."

Lois Lane turned her head toward Clark, who

was trying to hide the broken piece of heavy metal which he'd snapped like a match stick. A faint feeling stirred in her, as if she were caught in a strong wind suddenly blowing, high in space.

"You've broken the Bingo Jingo machine, Kent," said Perry White. "I can't thank you enough." He turned to Miss Henderson. "Send it back to the manufacturer."

"Mr. White, I *must* have the third number." She pointed her angular beak at the editor, squinted one eye, and something resembling a mongoose momentarily masked her face.

"Well, I can't turn the damn thing." White tapped the barrel.

"Excuse me, sir," said Kent, "but about that hometown reunion story—"

"Ok, Kent, the Prodigal Son returns. Go ahead, tell them you'll be there." He contemplated the Jingo machine. "Tell them *I'll* be there. Anything . . . but this . . . Jingo . . ."

Clark Kent turned away, happy to have been given the ok on the assignment. He became even happier a moment later, upon hearing Perry White say, "I just hope you realize it's not easy losing my top reporter."

A rash of happiness went down Clark Kent's neck, and a simpleton's grin crossed his face. A little recognition felt good once in a while. "Gee, thank you, Mr. White, that's—" He turned, only to find White addressing Lois Lane:

"You deserve the vacation, Lois."

"Oh," said Kent, crestfallen, "you're going away too?"

"Some of us go to Smallville," said Lois. "And some of us have to settle for—" She reached into a shopping bag and pulled out the world's tiniest bikini. "—Bermuda."

Clark Kent closed his eyes, slowly, and kept them closed. It would be madness to start up with Lois again; yes, she was slender and sexy, especially in the dress she was wearing today, and most certainly in her minuscule bathing suit. He opened his eyes. "That's a—charming bathing suit, Lois."

"Glad you like it, Clark." Lois twirled it on her finger. *Why do I lead him on like this? He's just a poor fish out of water . . .*

2

WEBCOE INDUSTRIES—DATA PROCESSING CENTER

Beyond these words, stenciled on a double-glass door, sat Gus Gorman. Gus's yo-yoing with computers had taken him into the heart of the industry, which recognized his peculiar knack with the instrument. Along the walls were massive data consoles, their tape decks alternately rolling and stopping, while other machines extruded printouts. Centered amongst the machines were the human controllers, Gus among them, fingers working, mind inside the enormous computer labyrinth.

Gus had a way with programs, could streamline them until they hummed like Hawaiian yo-yos.

But after all was said and done, he might as well be back on the street walking-the-doggie because he was *not* making the big money. Big money was floating by him on the screen, but when he reached for it, the little white numbers just danced away.

"... check ... here's your paycheck ..."

The payroll clerks were coming through, with their small-change wagon, the company payroll.

"Gus Gorman?"

Gus laid out his palm and his pay envelope was slapped into it. He slit the envelope open and tapped his check out, a look of dismay on his face. "Supposed to be two hundred twenty-five bucks a week, an' you know what this sucker say? One forty-three eighty."

The programmer next to him rotated in his chair. "Federal, state, and Social Security. That's so you'll still be getting money when you're sixty-five."

"Won't live to be sixty-five on one forty-three eighty," said Gus.

He rolled over to another console, check in his pocket, soul in turmoil. Other programmers rolled by in their own chairs, propelling themselves on ball-bearing wheels, from console to console. They were happy with $143.80 a week, for they liked goofing with the keyboard. But Gus needed a new yo-yo, one with rhinestones on it, and a golden thread ...

At lunchtime, as he strolled into the employees' cafeteria, money was still on Gus's mind. People were standing on line, waiting for the regular company fare—some plastic french fries and a piece of rubber cake. Gus shook his head, as he did each day when he got on line. "Seen some better eats than this in jail."

He shuffled along down the line, tray in front of him. At first, Gus had thought it would be good for his soul to be part of a big corporation, with his own ball-bearing chair. But this $143.80 a week was something else.

"Actually," said a colleague alongside him, "it's probably more like one forty-three eighty and one-half cent."

Gus took a dish of powdered mashed potatoes and some wood-fiber stew, then turned to his colleague. "How's that again?"

"There are always fractions left over in a paycheck, but they round it down to the lowest whole number."

"Never round it *up*, do they..." Gus suddenly understood. He looked at his fellow employees on line, hundreds of them in this shift, with more shifts to follow. "Everybody loses them fractions," he said, musing to himself.

"They don't actually lose 'em," said his colleague, a rounded-down little programmer with carrot-colored hair in his eyes. "They're floating around somewhere. The computer knows where they are."

Gus added a piece of vulcanized bread to his plate, but drifted on by the coffee machine. His colleague grabbed a cup for each of them. "How many sugars, Gus?"

"One—and a half," said Gus, watching the white cubes dissolve.

Computers know where all the half-cents have got to, reflected Gus, as he walked toward a long employee table, so reminiscent of mealtime in prison. *Long's I'm in jail,* thought Gus, *I might as well have stole somethin'* . . .

On a distant highway, a bus was making its way along, as buses will, by threatening anything smaller with its great gleaming snout. The passengers, numb from riding all day, watched dully as the scenery flopped past. Some read, while some slept fitfully, drooling on themselves. And still another, young Jimmy Olsen, yammered about life, photography, terminal acne, and anything else that came into his disordered mind. ". . . but my Uncle Al, on my father's side, he won't eat her stuffing . . ."

Clark Kent, seated beside Jimmy, stared blankly at him, as if he were a talking fish.

". . . he says it should be cooked outside the bird . . ."

Clark Kent could not help feeling that somehow Olsen had been cooked outside the bird, long ago.

". . . so my Aunt Grace told Aunt Ellen—Aunt Ellen's my father's half-sister . . ."

Clark Kent made polite noises, as the highway slipped by. The monotony of the horizon had dulled his thought processes and the stuffing saga had finished them. He felt like lifting the bus in the air and bringing it down where he wanted it, fast. *Patience,* said the inner voice. *You are, after all, immortal.*

Kent yawned, and looked past Olsen's head, out into the sky. Its long stretch of pale afternoon blue grew slowly red, for they were heading west; but the red, Kent noticed, was increasing, as if the sun had suddenly become tropic. And the bus was pulling over to the side of the road, flagged off by policemen manning the roadblock ahead.

Jimmy Olsen jumped from his seat. "We've got a story." The door opened and the bus driver stepped out. Olsen and Kent were behind him, as a state trooper gave the driver his choice:

"Turn back or wait until it's over."

"How long will that take?"

"You never know with a fire." The trooper turned toward the red glowing horizon.

"Just a fire?" The driver adjusted the belt over his large sagging stomach, as if to imply that he regularly drove his bus through a burning hoop.

"It's a chemical plant," the trooper now said to Clark Kent, who had flashed his press card. "Things could get hairy."

"Are there people in the plant?"

"Sure there are." The trooper gazed at the raging red clouds, as Jimmy Olsen scrambled into the bus and stepped back out with his camera. Secretively, he drew Clark Kent aside. "Keep them talking."

"Jimmy," said Kent, meekly, "it's dangerous."

Olsen gave him a superior smile; turkey stuffing

seemed to extrude from his ears. "Danger? That goes with the territory, Mr. Kent."

He raced off, as more and more vehicles were flagged down. Drivers jumped out of their cars excitedly, and Kent jumped into one smoothly, pausing only a moment in the backseat as he leapt from his three-piece into his uniform and came out the other door as—SUPERMAN!

Often as he'd done it, he always loved that first moment when he leapt into space and found himself flying; there would be a second's flash and he'd recall the great spiked-crystal ship that had brought him to Earth from Krypton; and then he was himself that flash, soaring.

He flew into the billowing red clouds. Their searing heat was lukewarm stuffing to Superman, but at the heart of the fire were people more flammable, and he saw them now, trapped upon the plant roof.

He whirled in flight, toward a gigantic aluminum chimney rising from the roof. With a graceful sidekick he toppled it neatly, forming a chute to the ground. The trapped employees raced toward it, climbed in, and slid down.

A startled crew of firemen watched the employees pop out the end of the chute, and then they saw *him,* circling in the flames, his own cape as red, and as brilliant. *He's got the answer,* thought the Fire Chief, *he always does*.

The elderly Chief wiped the water off his hat rim, and went back to directing the hoses, as people continued popping out of the chute, relief in their faces and gratitude on their lips.

"...a lawsuit like *they've* never seen before..."

"...terrible strawberry on my behind from that thing..."

The chute finally cleared the roof of people, but the Fire Chief's eye kept going to that section of the building his men had just pointed out to him— where the acid was kept.

Following this concern, he immediately had something else to worry about, because Jimmy Olsen was scurrying up the hook-and-ladder extension, into the raging clouds, two firemen chasing him.

"...hey, hey you jerk..."

"He'll cook himself up there."

They couldn't know that Olsen had been cooked outside the bird, and was too stupid to know fear. One hand on the ladder rung, the other on his camera, he climbed upward, giving it f.2 and other variations to adjust for the brilliant firelight that was burning the ends of his adolescent mustache.

"...Mr. White says a reporter *always* goes after a story..."

Incanting this bad advice to himself, he climbed higher, into the smoke.

Elsewhere in the building, a white-coated mad scientist stood in the center of a windowless laboratory, where he'd created, with government grants, the most devastating chemical substances imaginable, for use in baby food, drinking water, and perfumed towelettes. Nervously he watched a honeycombed grouping of white cannisters at the center of the room, the only room not yet devoured by flames, but through which smoke was slowly filtering.

"...I might have won a Nobel...but now..." He gazed protectively at his deadly cannisters. What was he to do?

"Sir, you'd better get out of here fast." Superman stood in the doorway, flames licking the hall behind him. "Come on, I'll show you the safest—"

"I can't leave." The mad scientist paced back and forth in front of his cannisters. He'd spent years here, perfecting his secrets and, owing to recent government legislation which would allow him to dump thousands of tons of chemical waste into a nearby river, was on the verge of yet another significant breakthrough. "That's concentrated Number Eight Beltric acid. If it heats up over one hundred and eighty degrees—" He wiped his brow. "—it will turn volatile. Clouds of it will rise—"

"Poison gas?"

"Once those acid clouds condense, they'll eat through concrete, steel, *anything*."

Flames were creeping now, through the doorway, and the walls of the windowless chamber were starting to crack and peel with the heat. The blue-green acid within the cannisters turned reddish, and a bubble or two appeared in the liquid. "It's—it's happening," said the chemist, face going pale.

The doorway filled with a fire crew, bearing a hose. "Stand back, we've got 'er..." The fireman manning the hose shouted down the hall. "... gimme the juice..."

A tiny trickle of water dribbled from the end of the hose. "... what the hell is this..."

"The water main broke!" A voice echoed through the smoke and the firemen looked at each other. Then everyone looked at the near wall, which burst into flames, mortar crumbling, studs burning, metal girders turning hot.

The mad scientist was staring at his bubbling cannisters. "... acid all over the Eastern seaboard..."

Superman turned, flew through the acrid cloud, to the grounds outside the building where the frenzied firemen were trying to coax their empty hoses. "Superman!" shouted the Chief. "I can't put this out without water!"

"Where's the nearest reservoir?"

"Five miles. We'll never make it."

Superman whirled, about to take the necessary steps, when he detected the groans of someone about to be flambéed. He flew back into the conflagration, and found Jimmy Olsen half conscious on the floor of the building, camera shattered, shoes melting. Superman scooped the youth into his arms and sped with him out to the emergency medical unit, his X-ray vision quickly scanning Olsen's leg. "It's a clean break, across the fibula."

The Man of Steel left the stunned medics behind, and soared into the air, above the building and the curtain of smoke and fire that enveloped it. His super-vision scanned the surrounding countryside, and came to rest upon the lake which the company had been polluting for years; not even a toad would go near it, but it would satisfy Superman's high purpose today.

Within his sublime form, incomprehensible chemical changes occurred, by which his breath turned unbearably cold; directing it at the lake he froze the entire basin of liquid. Then, flying down to the lake's edge, he gripped its now-frozen surface; with a single wrench he lifted the great sheet of ice into the air, a gleaming platter which he carried aloft.

"One frozen daiquiri . . . coming up . . ."

Balancing it on his up-raised palm, Superman sped back through the air with the platter of ice, and flung it down, into the burning plant. The ice melted, and smothered the flames. The building became a soggy, sizzling puddle. The bubbling acid cannisters cooled, and the mad scientist's eyes filled with tears of gratitude. His career, and the Eastern seaboard, had been saved. He turned to the Fire Chief. "It isn't very scientific to say it, but that man is a miracle." He turned to one of his staff in the lab. "And now—let's get back to work on that green mold."

"Miss Lane," said a press colleague at the airport in Bermuda, "it is a great pleasure to meet you . . ."

Lois turned in the blazing sun. Who were those two men following her?

3

A welcoming banner greeted Clark Kent as he approached the old schoolhouse, where he'd spent so many happy days of painful insecurity.

The maroon-and-white cloth fluttered in the evening breeze and Clark stood for a long moment gazing at it. Here he was, in Smallville once again. A choked feeling took him by the throat for here, in a certain sense, he'd been truly human, here, before his mission had come clear to him.

Smallville High, he said to himself, staring at its scarred brick facade. It said so much to him, this building. It said, *well look who's back—the class creep.*

"But all that's changed now," said Clark,

straightening his broad shoulders and adjusting his tie. "I've made it in Metropolis."

Why, you may be wondering, did the Man of Steel suffer these vague anxieties? Wasn't he, after all, able to leap over this building in a single bound?

The problem was, the role he'd played for so long, of bumbling blockhead, had solidified around him; he said and did things which weren't him at all, but which helped him get along, helped him to mingle with humanity. Did people need flattery? Fine, he'd flatter them. Did they need to feel superior to someone? Good, they could feel superior to him. Did they need someone to dump on now and then? Fine, they could dump on Clark Kent.

All of this had not left the Man of Steel unscarred.

He despised himself for all that mild-mannered stuff. Wouldn't it be wonderful to take a deep breath and blow Smallville High School into next month?

But no, he must go his way in silent humility, never letting them know that he could bend the school's iron gate over his forehead.

He walked slowly up the steps of the schoolhouse, ducked beneath the waving banner, and stepped through the doorway. Here was the old crowd, and they seemed, as always, to be enjoying themselves in ways mysterious to him—how easily they chatted, danced, and spread themselves around. He entered the room like a man rolling in on gumballs.

His steps were uncertain, the floor waxed to a dangerous gloss. Yes, it was the old gym alright, still echoing with cheers, yells, victory songs, and unbridled teenage violence. Smallville, oh Smallville, how dear you are to me . . .

Kent moved with uncertainty, feeling conspicuous, as if he'd arrived in his underwear, or wearing a rubber nose. The place was a blur, faces unrecognizable, but the tone was the same—of the in-crowd, laughing, on top of the world, while Clark Kent shuffled, muttered to himself, and adjusted his glasses with his index finger.

Music was playing, and bright chattering voices filled the air. Do I know these people, Kent asked himself? Did I *ever* know them?

The distance seemed as great as that between Earth and Krypton; and he realized that he'd always been concerned with other matters faintly sensed inside his strange form. Never had this laughter been his, nor these easy self-confident conversations. Always he'd brooded in secret about the meaning of universal life and immortality.

"Clark, why, Clark . . . Clark . . . something or other . . ."

He looked left, right, and then down—at a little old lady schoolteacher, face like a wrinkled partridge. Yes, it was she, Miss Bannister, Minnie as they used to call her, Mad Minnie.

" . . . yes, it is you, isn't it," she said. "I remember your essay on . . . on . . ."

Minnie fumbled with her beads, the same plastic cherries making the same clacking sound they'd made long ago. And she's as crazy now as she was then...

"You really have grown," she said, her eyes remembering nothing, the most fragmented person he'd ever known, given to chuckling to herself, skittering around the room like a windup penguin, talking incoherently, and always mislaying praise and blame. She'd been certifiably mad during his four years at Smallville and legend had it she'd always been openly psychotic—yet here she was, teaching high school English still.

"...but I take the stairs a bit slower," she said, changing the subject without warning, and making some strange mimicry of climbing stairs, in the same dress she'd worn seventeen years ago, a faded flower print that fluttered now, around her eccentric form. "...and of course I get these *spells*..."

Her spells, thought Kent, as it all came back to him. She'd been having spells back then. "You're looking well, Miss Bannister."

"...so many here tonight...paying me tribute..." She touched her thinning hair, which it'd been rumored she dyed with shoe polish, and Kent looked around, trying to figure an escape from the old zany. He found it in the eyes of Lana Lang.

"Will you excuse me, Miss Bannister? There's someone I have to say hello to."

He backed away from Minnie, who continued the conversation without him, gesturing to herself. He turned, and there was Lana, carrying a stack of records in one arm and a pile of paper plates in the other. Her red hair swung, her heels clicked efficiently, but she seemed a bit too efficient, as if to play down her solitary nature—the same solitary mantle Kent himself wore.

"Clark?" Her eyes questioned him, not quite sure if this tall modestly dressed fellow was the boy she'd known.

"Lana?"

"...I can't complain..." said Minnie Bannister, talking to herself alongside them. "...except for my spells..." She gestured to an invisible listener.

Kent and Lana Lang edged away from the madwoman. "You look wonderful, Lana," said Kent.

"So do you, Clark." Lana, for all her beauty, seemed unsure, here in the music of the golden oldies, beneath balloons and banners, here without a date, with just some long-playing records and paper plates in her arms. "Did you—come with anyone?"

"No, just me and—my shadow," said Kent.

They walked over to the DJ table, where the turntable was spinning, under the eyes of a discophile whose collection of bad music went back twenty years and more. He scanned his discs now, looking for one of those great old tunes, sung off-key by several aging delinquents. Yeah, here it is, this'll really grab them...

He hunched over his records as Lana and Clark approached, talking quietly to each other. Lana was nervous, for Clark had always attracted her in a strange bookish way; not much flash, but a solid

sort of guy. "...never thought I'd see *you* here..."
Her mind elsewhere, Lana put the stack of paper
plates down beside the turntable, and then headed
with her stack of records toward the buffet table.
These she placed beside the cold cuts. "...but
I'm so glad you *did* come, otherwise I'd be lost..."

"I heard you and Donald split up."

"Did you eat yet?" asked Lana, as if she hadn't
heard him, and took a record off the top of the
stack, preparing to ladle some potato salad onto it.
"Oh, that's not right. Hold this a sec, will you?"

She handed the ladle of potato salad to Clark,
picked up the records and took them back toward
the DJ table. Kent was left with the ladle and
stood contemplating it. Why was Lana so nervous?

"Hey, Kent, how're ya doing?"

A pair of alumni, with their wives, had spotted
Clark and came toward him now. These former
classmates were both enjoying material success,
their dress and style clear indicators of the rapid
advance they'd made in life; their hands came out
to shake Kent's. He extended the potato salad
ladle; then, seeing his error, quickly switched it to
his left hand.

"Hi, nice to see you again."

They smiled, in smooth superior fashion, and
looked at each other as if to say, *some guys never
change*. Clark Kent, a poor fool as always, made
them realize to even greater degree just how far
they'd come up in the world; they represented
prominent firms, dealt with big numbers, and
never shook hands with a potato ladle. "...like

you to meet our wives...Cynthia and Pauline
...Clark Kent, an old classmate..."

Kent tried to engage in some upwardly mobile
conversation, but the brittle smiles of the women
were too much for him; they looked on him as an
oaf, and consequently he acted like one, speaking too fast, inserting a finger in the chip dip,
and exhibiting a variety of nervous tics, one of
which, owing to his frequent clothing changes on
the run, was looking down to see if his fly was
open.

"Well, nice talking to you, Kent."

The couples backed away, obviously interested
in meeting more influential classmates than Clark
Kent, and leaving him where he was, alongside
the potato salad. Feigning indifference, he licked
off the chip dip and look around for Lana Lang.
His eyes fell instead on Brad Wilson, former
all-star quarterback, who was at that moment reliving
one of his great pass plays.

"...that game against Mid-City, that's the one
I'll never forget. Fourth quarter, score was tied..."

Brad Wilson's voice resembled that of a sports
announcer lost in enduring twilight; the game was
eternal and he thought the whole world was listening.
"...we're backed up on our own twenty-five-yard
line. The coach sends in a right flanker option..."

Clark Kent took the same option, flanking right
around Wilson, whose exploits he'd always found
boring; he himself could kick a football from the
twenty-five-yard line to the planet Mars but he'd
denied himself a career in high school and college

football, as it seemed a pointless exercise of his superhuman strength.

Avoiding Brad, he spotted Lana Lang again, who came toward him now, the same warm smile on her face. But Brad Wilson, defending against phantom tacklers, backpedaled, an invisible football in his hand and six martinis in his bloodstream to help him score. "... but I knew I could throw a long one..." He turned, looked downfield, and saw Lana. Thousands seemed to cheer him on as, bleary-eyed from booze, he walked toward her. Everlastingly self-crowned as he was, in helmet and victory wreath, he greeted her.

"Here I am, honey, and I'm all yours. Remember when you were Queen of the Prom? All the guys had to get in line to dance with you." He took her arm and swiveled her toward the music.

"I can't," she said. "I've promised Clark."

Brad Wilson turned and looked toward Kent, who stood before him now, the water boy. Wilson's brow knitted into a frown, and he contemplated giving Kent the old stiff-arm. "Hiya, Kent, long time no see. Not that you ever could." He pointed at Kent's glasses.

"Hello, Brad, you're looking—well." Clark gazed at Wilson's booze-swollen jowels.

The former golden boy swayed on his ever-present twenty-five-yard line and smirked at Kent. "I'm feelin' good too. I'm still callin' the plays." He gestured vaguely, as if to indicate a huddle of men around him, ready to steamroll the world at his command. He was, in fact, distributor of a

local beer; the taste of this brew, resembling
boiled gym shoes, was popular with the bums
around the courthouse square, and in cellar tav-
erns where old athletic supporters went to die
from drinking it. "I'm always looking into the
end zone, Kent, for an open receiver. Know
what I mean?"

Kent nodded, though no one, including Wilson
himself, knew what he meant, but such vague
allusions to the game of life gave Wilson the
feeling that his every move was on network TV.
Let it be said for the man that he did coach in the
Weener League, warping the outlook of youths
from ages eight to twelve, every Saturday. "...and
when I throw that long one, Kent, when I let it fly,
I know somebody's going to be there to catch it."

Nobody was there to continue listening though,
for as Wilson sidestepped an imaginary tackler,
Clark and Lana Lang moved onto the dance floor,
arm in arm.

"I didn't remember that you danced," said
Lana softly.

"I don't," said Kent, who could have danced a
supersonic Spanish fandango if he cared to, or
performed an old soft-shoe routine upside down on
the ceiling. However, he masked these talents as
he masked all his others, and led Lana in a
shuffling little two-step, which sufficed to carry
them deeper onto the dance floor, away from
Wilson. The music settled around them gently and
they moved easily together, each wondering what
the night could bring.

I mustn't let it happen, thought Clark Kent. I'm from Krypton and she's from Earth.

But the band was playing Earth Angel . . .

Surrounded by gigantic beasts of steel and silicon, Gus Gorman processed his data, storage compartments zinging out their information. His colleague, carrotish hair in his eyes, wheeled on by him. "I love this company," he said. From a distance came the sound of the payroll wagon. "The dress code has taught me how to dress, the management team has taught me how to sing, and I love this number cruncher." He patted the Big Machine, as Gus shook his head slowly. Carrot Head's mind was stacked wrong somehow; definitely not an advanced system like Gus's.

". . . and you can get ahead in this company," continued his colleague, "if you learn to play tough." He winked at Gus and took a ballpoint pen from the vinyl nerd-pouch inserted in his pocket. He waggled the tip of the ballpoint toward Gus. "Know what I mean?"

"Sure do, baby," said Gus, wheeling his own chair around, as the payroll wagon came nearer.

"Of course," said his colleague, "I don't mind being in the fishbowl, but Management is where you make the big money."

"So I've heard," said Gus softly, as the wheels of the wagon clicked nearer.

"Sure, I like programming, and I'm an engineer at heart, but Management—" The carrot-haired colleague tapped his nose with the ballpoint. "—that's the Goal."

"Expense accounts and flyin' around," nodded Gus. "I can see you now."

His colleague smiled warmly at this image, and inserted his ballpoint back in his nerd-pouch with a managementlike flourish. The glass doors of the fishbowl opened and the uniformed payroll team wheeled their carts inside. Envelopes with paychecks nestled within were distributed.

"Should be another one there for Walter J. Morris," said Gus. He smiled at the payroll clerk. "He put in an expense voucher."

The clerk looked again, brought out a second envelope. "Where is he?"

"Don't worry," said Gus. "He's on the computer. I'll give it to him."

In this fashion, a check for $85,789.80 was handed over to Gus, who was also goal-oriented.

The dance had ended, the gym was empty. Mad Minnie Bannister had been escorted home by an hallucination, and Brad Wilson had gone over to the old football field where so much glory had been his; there, deep in his own end zone, he threw a long one, and then threw up. Clutching a padded goalpost, he sank to the ground and fell asleep. The old school grounds were silent. But from the gym the strains of Earth Angel came once more, softly.

The windows of the gym were faintly lit; inside,

taking down the streamers, were Lana Lang and Clark Kent, each one mounted on a ladder.

"Thank you for helping me out," said Lana, her voice echoing in the big empty space.

On the other ladder, at the far side of the gym, Clark turned, crepe paper draped on both his shoulders. He gazed at Lana, as she stretched above her to untie a streamer. "There must be a lot of guys, Lana, who'd like to be in my shoes right now."

"You'd be surprised how many offers I *didn't* get," said Lana, confetti in her hair, a balloon bouncing gently off her head and falling to the floor. "Even Brad wouldn't stick around for this."

Brad, of course, was now asleep on the football field, dreaming of naked cheerleaders, who covered him in pom-poms.

Lana reached above her again, trying to untack a long crepe-paper banner. "It's really difficult."

"The streamers?" Clark gave a tug. "They're no problem. You just pull at them and—"

"Not the streamers," said Lana. "Everything."

"Is—something wrong, Lana?" Clark turned, balloons descending slowly around his ladder, onto the empty bandstand below.

"I'm not complaining," said Lana. "It's just that—" She paused, and gazed back at him across the gym floor. "Why do I feel I can talk to you?"

"What?" asked Clark, straining to hear through a veil of crepe paper.

"I feel like I can talk to you!" shouted Lana, her voice echoing among the rafters of the gym.

A silly grin crossed Clark's face. "Well, I always wished you would talk to me. Back when you were—"

Lana reached up, to take down a large photo the Reunion Committee had hung, of herself as Queen of the Prom. Beside her in the photo was the King, the young man she'd fallen in love with on the night of the Senior Prom. "The Royal Couple," said Lana, gazing at herself and the boy who'd become her husband, owing to the romantic atmosphere of that night of nights—the soft lights, the music, the streamers, the breaking balloons, one of which had broken in the backseat of the young man's car toward dawn in Lovers' Lane.

". . . and three years after the Royal Wedding," said Lana, climbing down her ladder, "the King abdicated. Isn't that terrible?" She turned away from Clark, toward the buffet table.

"It certainly is," said Clark compassionately, climbing down his own ladder.

"There must be a gallon of potato salad left," said Lana, shaking her head at the waste. "You know what the problem is?"

Clark stepped in beside her. "Too much mayonnaise?"

"Donald loved mayonnaise," said Lana, glancing back at the photo of her ex-husband and then at Kent. "Why would you think that was the problem?"

"I didn't—" Kent broke off, confused by her skipping thoughts, her eyes, her perfume.

"The problem is," said Lana, "why do I stay in

Smallville?'' She stared at Clark, her voice growing heated. ''I've asked myself that question a hundred times. Do you know how lucky you are to live in Metropolis?''

Clark met her gaze through his thick lenses. How pretty she was, with something very humble about her, unlike Lois Lane who was so self-confident, and cutting as a chain saw. Have I cured myself of Lois, only to find—Lana? ''There's room for everybody in Metropolis, Lana. You could—''

''That's easy for you to say. But how?'' Lana's voice turned wistful. ''And what about Ricky?''

''Ricky?''

''My little boy. At least here we've got a house. And I've got a job. Ok, I'm just a secretary, but it pays the bills.''

''I'm sure you're not just a secretary, Lana.''

''Yes, I'm also errand girl and talking coffee-pot.'' She looked at the photograph again, of herself in her cardboard crown. ''And I was once Royalty.'' She sighed and pulled another streamer down. ''And last winter when fuel went up I had to pawn my diamond ring.''

''I'm sorry.''

''Well, there's nothing I can do about *that*.''

Clark started to put a comforting arm around her, then realized she was no longer talking of the lost ring, but about a cluster of balloons floating far above the rafters of the gym. ''Unless,'' she said, nodding toward them, ''we could fly up and get them.''

Kent gave a fleeting, private smile. The temptation was there as always, to reveal himself, to float off the ground, to fly to the rafters, to lift the building, balance it on one finger and then lay it at Lana's feet. Yes, he thought, I'm falling again. He must watch himself; it was astonishing the way a woman of Earth got inside you; before you knew it, her mirror was in your mind and the night became her face. Lana Lang was already there, her soft nature somehow moving through him, making faint suggestions that seemed to come from a star, yet were actually dangerously near, close as the scent of her maddening perfume. She was glancing at him now, some mischief in her eyes.

"You never married?"

Kent shrugged. "I came close." The folly of past intimacy with Lois Lane pricked his conscience now; he'd thrown his great strength away like an old suit, for the sake of one night's embrace, for the feeling of being just a man, not Superman. That was the law—that if he truly loved a mortal woman he must forsake his cosmic power. Gladly had he forsaken it for Lois Lane, and the very next day a truck driver had beaten the living crap out of him.

No, he must not let *that* happen again.

But the music, that enchanting theme, again whispered to him, Earth Angel.

And Lana's eyes had traveled now, to the photograph of another youth hanging above them, that of young Clark Kent, squinting myopically toward the camera, in a class picture taken long ago, when he was water boy. "You know," said Lana quietly, "years later you can look at someone and think, well, I guess that's the one, that's the one who got away."

Careful, said Kent to himself, the moonlight is weaving itself around us.

"Did someone get away from *you*, Clark?" Lana turned toward him.

"Yes, Lana, they did." He touched her wrist gently. "My dog ran away."

Lana looked at him, an eyebrow slightly raised. Could she be all wrong about Clark Kent? Were the streamers, the balloons, the music deceiving her again? Was he actually a nincompoop?

They stuffed streamers into a big cardboard box, each wondering about the other, while outside Brad Wilson slept between the goalposts, alcohol circulating through his system and causing the naked cheerleaders to lead him across a burning desert where he gasped with thirst, a blinding pain in his temples. At dawn he would wake, feeling he'd swallowed a pom-pom.

But now the moonlight shown gently upon him, and upon Smallville High itself, and on Minnie Bannister whose madcap teaching style had given complexes to all her students; she'd found her way home somehow, and crawled into her bed, after stabbing around underneath it with a broom. Staring at the ceiling, she recited the alphabet and closed her eyes. I'm Queen of the Prom, she said to herself, and perhaps she was.

The moonlight slanted through her window, and

through all the windows of Smallville, where Superman had spent his youth. This town held the moon's greatest secret, and the secret of a farther star, the sun of long-dead Krypton. The secret played in the silvery beams of light, and in the rustling leaves.

Two figures left the Smallville gym, and walked together through the empty streets . . .

4

Webcoe Industries, which employed Gus Gorman,
was run by Ross Webster, Humanitarian of the
Year. "I like to call my servants by their first
name," was one of his frequent humanistic re-
marks. His office was a sleek playroom at the top
of Webcoe, the walls made of silvery steel connected to a large clear dome directly over his desk.
Gazing out through this dome, he would think
about humanity, his principle thought being how
he could sell it something it didn't want or need.

Computer games flashed in three corners of the
metallic room, and a large piece of high-tech
sculpture ticked and clicked in the fourth, levers
moving, pendulums swinging, wires glowing, none

of it performing anything useful, thus making it an effective symbol of Webcoe Industries.

Ross Webster's genial face had formed itself into a stern mask, and he looked across his desk at the Chief Accountant of Webcoe, a Mr. Simpson, whose spirit Webster had crushed decades ago.

"Give me that again, fella," said Webster, leaning forward in his chair. "Run that by me one more time."

Simpson, whose Adam's apple was moving nervously up and down, shaped his words fearfully. "Eighty-five thousand . . . dollars . . ."

"Missing?"

"Embezzled, Mr. Webster. Stolen from the firm."

"Simpson," said Webster, "I run this company on indigestion and profit. *Your* indigestion and my profit. Are you trying to tell me someone has reversed that equation? *My* indigestion and *their* profit?"

"I—I don't know, sir. I've been beside myself all day trying to understand."

Ross Webster came slowly from his chair. He was a gruff man, yes, but he carried himself with a democratic air. His stern mask changed now to a comradely smile and, as he laid a hand gently on Simpson's shoulder, his voice had once again grown calm. "Simpson, I want you to find out who this individual is. If you don't, you'll be transferred to Beirut." Webster gave Simpson's shoulder an encouraging little squeeze. "Is that clear?"

"Yessir."

"Good, Simpson, excellent." The Humanitarian of the Year released his friendly grip on Simpson's shoulder and mused to himself, as he shook his head back and forth. "Eighty-five thousand dollars . . . stolen . . ."

"*By whom?*" A strident female voice rang out from the anteroom. Milk, which Mr. Simpson drank for his bleeding ulcer, curdled in his glass as Vera Webster, Ross Webster's sister, entered the office. Perry White of the *Daily Planet* had observed upon seeing a photograph of her that she was a trained spinster. He'd failed to add that she also bore an unfortunate resemblance to Joseph Stalin. Had she a mustache, history might never have pronounced him dead. "*Stolen by whom?*" she repeated, charging across the office toward her brother and Simpson. "That's what I want to know. By whom?"

"Get hold of yourself, Vera," said Ross Webster. And then to himself, *Nobody else ever will.* For years he'd been trying to marry her off to Arab royalty, then to any sort of millionaire, and finally even to Simpson, who refused, preferring bookkeeping in Beirut to Vera.

She charged at the poor devil now. "Eighty-five thousand dollars! It's outrageous. Who did it? Who?"

"I don't know," said Simpson, cringing like the broken snail he was. Then, bile flaring up, he snarled bitterly. "In the old days we kept *books,* we had *ledgers,* we could see what was coming in and what was paid out. If somebody wanted to rob

71

you, he'd come in with a gun and say stick 'em up! Nowadays they get these blasted computers to do their dirty work!"

"Simpson," said Ross Webster, "you are Yesterday. Whoever pulled this caper is Tomorrow."

Vera Webster frowned in disgust at both men; life, having given her a face like Joseph Stalin, completed the job by making her impatient to the point of aggression. She looked ready to bite a desk, or kick poor Simpson in the sensitive area of his stomach. She might have done these things, were it not for the stunning entrance of Loreli Ambrosia.

Loreli looked nothing like Joseph Stalin, and this alone would have made Vera Webster dislike her. Added to this, however, was Loreli's position in the company, which Vera was inclined to view as a prone one, on her brother's office couch. "What do *you* want?" Vera gave Loreli a withering stare, but Loreli ignored it and walked over to Webster.

"Ross, honey, it's time for your massage." Loreli placed her two hands gently on the back of Webster's neck. "You know how good it makes you feel."

"Yes, of course."

Vera Webster goose-stepped forward. "How dare you let this woman burst into a sensitive conference like this!"

"I give a *very* sensitive massage," said Loreli, rubbing Ross's neck.

"Yes," said Webster, "it relaxes me in times of crisis."

Vera stationed herself in front of Loreli and barked as if addressing troops at Leningrad. "We're trying to hold a meeting here!"

"Try holding your breath," said Loreli, sweetly.

"Pay attention," said Vera, turning toward Simpson. "I am about to take a human life."

Simpson, who wished someone would take Vera out and prune her, could only stare at his curdled milk.

"Ross," shrieked Vera, "I will not have this woman insulting me."

"Tell her," countered Loreli, "to stop insulting *me!*"

Ross Webster intervened, respecting the human values of each. "Mouths closed! Ears open! I can't have anyone with me who isn't with me!"

What leadership, thought Simpson, who'd seen Vera bite lesser men on the earlobe; but she cowered before Ross Webster, for reasons unknown to Simpson; in her youth Vera's brother had, obeying one of his first humanitarian instincts, tortured her unmercifully with an early electronic project kit, which caused her hair to stand on end for hours. The memory of this, and other projects, subdued her now. "I'm sorry, Ross."

"That's better," said Webster. "Now kiss and make up."

"I don't kiss," said Vera.

"Well then, shake hands."

The two enemies shook hands, their knuckles turning white, but Loreli managed a smile and Vera showed a bit of tooth as well as some gum. Ross Webster nodded his satisfaction, for he liked to be surrounded at all times by the illusion of good will. "That's my best gals." He turned back toward Simpson. "Well, chum, what now? Kiss that eighty-five thou good-bye? Pay some thief's salary while he thinks up new ways to shake the money tree?"

"He's bound to slip up sooner or later," said Simpson limply.

"He won't slip up at all," said Ross Webster, pacing between the others. "He'll just go on quietly taking the bread from our mouths. He'll keep a low profile and won't do a thing to call attention to himself—unless he's an utter moron."

A roaring sound from the company parking lot caused the group to move as one to the window. They stared openmouthed as a bright red Ferrari zoomed down one of the lanes, executed a hairpin turn, burnt rubber, and slipped into a parking place.

The car door opened and Gus Gorman stepped out, spinning the Ferrari keys on his finger. ". . . lookin' cool, babe . . ." he said to his reflection in the gleaming window of the new machine. He turned toward the Webcoe tower, its glass exterior casting an even brighter reflection. "an' nobody suspect a goddamn thing . . ."

Ross Webster stared down at this audacious figure walking across the parking lot he'd built with unskilled nonunion labor. "Who is that character?"

Gus walked with a rolling gait, yo-yo whizzing off his finger, the Ferrari keys still spinning too. "I beat these people to death with this move . . ." He yo-yoed along toward the Webco tower, figuring he'd just duck in and make one more payroll deduction, after which he'd vanish from sight.

". . . everything happenin' right on schedule . . ." He entered and walked to the elevator, snapping his fingers and humming to himself, the world around him seeming to be in slow motion, with himself ahead of it.

The world, like the good computer it was, was ticking every 220-billionth of a second, with all kinds of moves, but they were just smoke rings to Gus. ". . . ahead of them dudes by so far . . ."

He chuckled to himself, and stepped into the elevator, lost in his own thoughts, seeing none of the other folks there, who nonetheless found his new alligator-skin pants somewhat strange for the corporation.

Gus was a happy guy, intensely in his own dream, but it *wasn't the dream everybody else was having.*

They were Webcoe employees.

They punched timeclocks.

They rolled around with mechanical regularity on their ball-bearing chairs.

Gus, seeing straight suits and trimmed hair, and a row of plastic heads, thought to himself, *these dudes can't even see me.*

His yo-yo went down, its tiny rag polishing his shoe tips.

All eyes in the elevator were upon this act.

...I just *glide* on by these folks...

Gus hummed and snapped his fingers to a distant beat, the presence of everyone else in Webcoe no more than a silvery transparent shadow...

...while incredible computer music went through his head...

His lips moved, making strange buzzing sounds. Other mock computer noises followed, as he sang to himself, 220 billion moves ahead of *this* day, which he had *in* hand.

That a man should play with a yo-yo in the elevator of Webcoe was, of course, unheard of.

Gus's yo-yo had a battery in it, causing it to light.

His fellow employees watched this illuminated object going up and down.

...got these people hyp-notized...

Gus's lighted yo-yo was equipped with a microwire that emitted a one-note tune, around which Gus improvised some mouth-saxophone runs, as the Webcoe employees watched from inside their plastic heads, eyeballs clicking.

...got 'em so jived they can only see my *outline*...

Clicking his fingers, spinning his yo-yo, he watched the elevator open at his floor, and stepped off.

He checked his watch. "...payroll wagon due by any minute..."

He'd collect his final check, for $143.80. It wasn't much, and maybe Gus should have left it behind. But he'd seen a pair of suede socks he wanted to buy, and a tasteful little belt made of boa-constrictor lips.

5

Far away in Smallville, a number of young people had gathered at the bowling alley. They were just Smallville kids, and like so many boys their age all over America, were sadists. Two team captains had just picked sides, and the last little bowler to be chosen was Ricky Lang, Lana Lang's timid son. One of the team captains looked at him now, and sneered. "I guess I have to take this wimp."

"Too bad for you," mocked the other team captain, whose father owned the largest unethical law firm in town.

"Well," sighed the other captain, "let's go." He shoved Ricky toward his teammates who, in typical small-town American fashion would try to dominate and destroy his will by whatever means occurred to them.

"I just can't stand this," said Lana Lang, watching from the scoreboard table.

"He'll be alright," said Clark Kent. "I should know, Lana. I was a late bloomer myself."

At the bowling alley bar, several other late bloomers were having a sociable drink or two. "I bowled shum boo'tiful games'hin thish placesh..." said one of them, twirling his swizzle stick.

"... shay lissen..." His companion waggled a finger. "... I've sheen you do it..."

Neither of them had ever bowled anything but beer bottles since the day they were born. Seated beside these distinguished athletes was Brad Wilson, enjoying a few drinks himself, his libido rising slowly at the sight of Lana Lang, until he finally swaggered from the bar and strolled toward her, to the sound of falling tenpins.

"Hiya, sweet thing." He pointed toward her son, Ricky. "Little guy's gettin' hassled, is he?" Wilson looked down at Clark Kent. "You still hangin' around?"

"I seem to be," said Clark, mildly.

Wilson looked back toward the group of boys, who were mocking Ricky Lang as he tried to finger the bowling ball. Wilson bent close to Lana. "All that kid needs is a couple of pointers from the ol' champ here." He looked toward Kent. "I bet you didn't know I won the all-county bowling trophy two years in a row."

"No, I didn't know that, Brad."

"A natural athlete can play any sport."

With that he turned and walked toward Ricky Lang.

"Oh no," said Lana to Clark Kent, "this will only make it worse."

The delicate youth was struggling to lift the bowling ball, arms trembling, knees wobbling, lower abdomen straining toward an early hernia. Gamely he took his position, staggered forward to the line and released the ball, which bounced and then rolled weakly into the gutter.

"See," said an encouraging member of Ricky's peer group, "he's a fruit."

Ricky's ears burned; another neurotic patch was starting to sew itself to his character, and Brad Wilson was coming forward to make certain the patch would hold like iron. Such was his coaching style, beloved in the community. "Hey, sport, you're holdin' it all wrong. Lemme show you—"

Ricky was struggling with another ball, as his teammates continued snickering. Brad attempted to wrest the bowling ball from Ricky's hand, causing the boy's thumb to bend dangerously near the snapping point. "Let ol' Uncle Brad show you how it's done."

"Say, Brad," said a quiet voice at his elbow, "I think he'll be better off doing it his own way."

Brad turned, boorish surprise in his face. "For a guy who was lucky to be water boy on the team, you sure have a big mouth, Kent."

At the bowling alley bar, the two drunks pivoted on their stools. "Shay . . . looksh like those two might get into a boxin' match . . ."

"I ushta box all over thish county," said the other, who'd been beaten senseless by everyone he'd ever raised his voice to, in or out of the ring.

At the bowling lanes, Clark Kent was lowering his voice, attempting to spare Ricky any embarrassment. "I think Ricky would rather not get a bowling lesson in front of the other kids."

"He needs a *man* to show him," countered Wilson, hinting that Clark Kent was not a man but rather some kind of potted flower.

Kent ignored the slur. "Ricky will do fine on his own." He turned to the boy. "Give it your best shot, Ricky."

Ricky withdrew from the two men and staggered once again toward the line. Clark Kent turned back toward Lana, giving her a reassuring smile, and then proceeded to trip over the resin container. Chalk rose in the air, as Ricky released his second ball. The ball bounced feebly toward the tenpins. Clark Kent, with chalk in his nose, let out a sneeze.

It was no ordinary sneeze.

A tremendous gust of wind came from his godlike nostrils, dove in behind the bowling ball, and drove it with invisible force straight down the lane. The ball, traveling at superspeed, hit the pins and shattered them like china cups; all of them went down and the pinboy had to jump for his life as the ball crashed into the pit.

"Wow," said Ricky's peers, drawing back in fear from the frail companion they'd been tormenting.

"Gesundheit," said Lana.

"Thank you," said Clark Kent, taking out his handkerchief.

Gus Gorman worked his computer console, as white dots and lines flew across an electronic field of blue. "Payroll wagon seem to be late today," said Gus to himself, as he listened for the faraway wheels.

His colleague, the carrot-headed programmer, looked toward Gus. "Were you talking to me?" he inquired pleasantly.

"Been listenin' for the cash car," said Gus, cupping one hand behind his ear. "Don't seem to hear it comin'."

"No, of course it's not coming," said the carrot-top. "Today's not payday."

"Not payday?" Gus quickly worked his computer keyboard, to confirm what day it was, and realized that some parts of his program were out of sync.

The lovely floating quality he'd been enjoying on his ball-bearing chair turned rocky. He clutched. A second later, the door to the fishbowl opened and a department head stuck his face inside. "Gus, the boss wants to see you."

"Which boss that?"

"*The* boss."

Gus swallowed with difficulty. Dark feelings surfaced in his mind, long hidden but all too familiar, of having screwed up again. "The . . . the . . . the . . ." He stammered nervously, and rolled backward in his chair; an ominous sense came over him, that the building was now filled with cops, investigating fraud and embezzlement. "...b...b...b...boss?"

He fumbled with his yo-yo, his moron-mode clicking on, made of a thousand insecurities, principally his memory of being in jail, a place he did not want to visit again, ever. He felt, momentarily, more stupid than a chimpanzee, his yo-yo bobbing up and down accordingly, as his mind fell apart. Ohgodohgod notjailagain ohno...

He spun around in his chair and pedaled away through the rows of data machines, whose red and black squares seemed suddenly like a monstrous chess board....ohmygodoh god...

He pedaled along, further astonishing his already amazed fellow programmers, for travel on ball-bearing chairs was never used to quite the extent Gus was trying to use it, as a means to go out the door, down the hallway, into the elevator, and across the parking lot.

...got to make some *time* with this chair, got to outwheel them suckers...

Thus, Gus, pedaling his way through the three-dimensional chess board of the massive computer files; he circled there, until it finally occurred to him that he was acting a trifle odd.

At the doorway, where the department head stood frowning, Gus rose from his chair; it sailed on without him, as he straightened the seams in his alligator pants. "Boss want to see me? Mr. Ross Webster himself?"

"You'd better move it," said the department head.

Outside the door, two company security guards were waiting, bulldog smiles on their faces. "Right this way, Gus."

Takin' me away. I got to make a break for it, but if I do these jazzbos *will* shoot me in the back.

Very leas' jump on my kidneys and transplant them to the end of my spine.

"Sure, fellas, let's go," said Gus, swaggering confidently, but his yo-yo betrayed him, string dangling, yo-yo losing speed. "Say, how you boys like to wait one second while I hop in the restroom?"

"Mr. Webster don't like to be kept waiting."

Gus looked at each of the guards, whose faces were like pink hamhocks. Revolver holsters creaked and Gus found himself counting all the little silver bullets in the gun belts. Against them he had only his great but undependable speed, which might or might not carry him like a greased eel under the elevator door and down the shaft.

The guards led him by the elbows, as the elevator door opened. "Goin' up, Gus," they said, and helped him in.

Goin' *to* jail.

The elevator door closed. Other Webcoe employees riding the elevator saw a man whose yo-yo was hanging motionless from the end of his finger, said, finger extended in the air.

"Ross the Boss?" He looked at the security guards.

They nodded, smiling.

Gus managed a sickly smile of his own, his yo-yo arm remaining outstretched, bent at the elbow.

The elevator continued upward, a smooth whirring sound coming from the shaft, which Gus realized he was about to get.

Goin' to be runnin' the prison computer.

So now's the time for me to make my break, when these doors open. I'll leap out like a goddamn jackrabbit an' get myself shot in both of my ass cheeks.

Gus stepped quietly, onto that floor of Webcoe occupied by its owner and president, toward whose office he was now directed, with a nightstick in his back.

"Mr. Gorman?" asked a secretary sweetly. "Mr. Webster is waiting to see you."

"Say, where's the washroom at? I'd like to fresh up my face a little . . ."

. . . climb out the window, slide down the side of the building, glide like a bat, land in the bushes, creep along somewhere till it gets dark, then faaaade.

"Is he here yet, Miss Collins?" barked the intercom.

"Yes, sir," said Miss Collins, pushing the intercom button. "I'm sending him in."

The security guards escorted Gus forward, opened the door to Webster's office, and sent him through. Gus went, yo-yo dead and dragging along the carpet from his limp trailing arm.

Ahead of him was Ross Webster, seated behind his massive desk. "Mr. August Gorman?"

Gus looked at the bright steel walls, and felt them closing in on him with a *clang*.

"Please, Mr. Webster, you know what it's like in jail?" Gus gestured with his lifeless yo-yo. "You send an innocent man in with them robbers and rapers and killers an' he come out someday and kill *you*."

Ross Webster toyed with a gold-tipped pen. "Mr. Gorman, you've been a naughty guy." Webster gave a congenial laugh. Warm feelings of humanitarianism streamed through this laughter, causing Gus Gorman to feel his socks falling down with fear; he'd known a prison warden who used to smile in that same friendly way before he put you in solitary to sleep on concrete in your underpants.

"Mr. Webster, please, don't do whatever it is you're thinkin' of doin'." Gus came forward, yo-yo bouncing on Webster's rug.

Webster continued in his gentle smiling way as if Gus had only taken a few paper clips. "C'mon now, admit it, you've been kinda naughty."

Gus felt his eyes starting to water. The man was toying with him, the way the warden used to before locking him in the cement closet for six weeks, with only his battery-powered yo-yo to see by.

Ross Webster rose and walked to the bookcase behind his desk. He lightly touched the spine on one of the volumes shelved there, and the entire bookcase rotated, revealing a complete wet bar on the other side. "I understand, Gus. I know where you're coming from.'' Webster poured himself a drink. ''You want to be rich, right?''

Gus stared at Webster, visions of concrete mattresses still filling his mind; he heard the long cell block ringing in his brain and seemed to taste again the special flavor of prison beans.

Gonna be eatin' that food again.

Unless I leap up, bust through that glass dome, and parachute to the ground below.

Seem like a good plan.

''Now me,'' said Webster, ''I was born rich. I've never worn the same pair of socks twice.''

''What do you do with them?''

''I believe they're laundered and sent to some charitable institution. I don't know what happens to them then. Maybe they use them for dust rags or pen wipers.''

''Or socks.''

''Yes, that never occurred to me.'' Webster handed Gus a drink. ''Here you go, buddy, single-malt, you'll love it.'' Webster smiled again. ''Gus, my friend, you're a genius. A naughty genius, but hell, nobody's perfect.''

Gus chugalugged the drink and stared at Webster again. ''Because I know about gettin' those half-cents?''

''Because computers run the world today—'' Webster began to speak as if addressing a gathering of humanitarians, and strode back and forth in the room, gesturing grandly. ''—and the fellow who can fool the computers will run the world.''

As Webster spoke, Gus grew more comfortable.

Man's got the soul of a thief.

Gus walked over to the bar and poured himself another drink. He turned, leaning an elbow on the bar. It rotated, and carried him into the wall.

Darkness filled his eyeballs, and the drink rattled in his hand.

Solitary confinement, right in his office. This man is *slick*.

"*...I've been searching for a long time for somebody who can make these machines do things they're not supposed to. Do you catch my drift?*"

Webster's voice came through the wall. Gus called for help, but Webster was staring out over the company grounds and did not know Gus was locked in the wall.

"...yes, I know you're the man for this. You have a light touch, you nearly escaped detection. With the full power of my organization behind you, there's no limit to what you might do..."

Gus thrashed about in the bar, turning on water taps, cracking ice cubes, beating his head against the interior wall. Finally he located the switch and found himself swinging back out into the room, as Ross Webster turned and strode toward the office door.

"Gus, the Webster industrial complex owns a little magnesium here, a little zinc there. Over here some railroads, over there some farm machinery. You follow?"

Gus was hurrying across the carpet after him. "I'm tryin' to."

Ross turned in his tracks. "Gus, do you know what I want now? I want coffee."

Gus pivoted, his delivery-boy mode on. "Black or regular?"

"I don't think you understand," said Ross, taking Gus by the elbow in a comradely fashion as they resumed their march through the corridor. "Under different company names I control the price of coffee beans in Brazil, Venezuela, Java, Bolivia, and the Republic of Gabon."

Gus nodded, and worked his yo-yo thoughtfully, life returning to the precision instrument, its rainbow whirling again. This dude, thought Gus, is offerin' me some kind of deal whereby he will use my peculiar talent, and then rotate me back into the wall.

But I wasn't born yesterday, Jack.

I will rotate *him* into the wall.

And slip out the back door 'bout a million dollars richer than I am right now.

". . . but y'see," droned Webster, "the problem I have is that one country just won't play ball with me. You know how that can bug a guy, don't you?"

"Absolutely. Country don' play ball with you, it can ruin breakfast, lunch, an' dinner." Gus narrowed his gaze. "Which country is it?"

"Colombia," said Webster, his face darkening. "Oh, I tried to reason with them—" He gestured with the noble air he'd shown at the Humanitarian of the Year banquet, a gesture displaying greatness of heart and boundless patience. "So now I wipe them out."

"Wipe them out?"

"Destroy the entire Colombian coffee crop down to the last bean."

"The las' bean? You sure you can't just let this one little old country do their own thing?"

"A very wise man once said—I think it was Attila the Hun—it's not enough that I succeed. Everyone else must fail." Webster put an arm around Gus's shoulder. "And do you know how I'm going to do it, Gus?"

"The weather!" The voice of Vera Webster shattered the atmosphere. A moment later she turned the corner, in front of Gus.

Bitch look like Stalin, thought Gus to himself. "Hey, lissen," he said, turning to Ross Webster, "I didn't know your mama was comin'."

"I'm his *sister,*" snapped Vera Webster, epaulets on her militaristic suit rising as she lifted her shoulders to attention. "His *baby* sister."

Gus's alligator pants seemed to stir, interested in Vera. *Take it easy,* said Gus. Lady has teeth and scales but she ain't no crocodile. Is she?

Ross Webster spoke: "Gus, tell me, have you ever heard of Vulcan?"

Gus looked at Vera. "That what they call you?"

Vera's epaulets swelled higher. Her posture, reminiscent of a drill sergeant Gus used to know, grew stiffer. She moved toward him, speaking through her teeth. "Vulcan is the weather satellite our government put up in orbit to monitor the weather."

"But if somebody reprogrammed it," said Ross Webster, "it could do much more."

"It could make weather!" Vera Webster smiled, her narrow-set and beady eyes shining with the sort of thing Gus saw in her brother's eyes too—wealth that walks the Earth, making big moves.

These people are heavy dudes.

I've come a long way in five minutes, ain't I.

"Weather!" repeated Vera. "We can control the sky."

"Storms! Floods!" Ross Webster gestured, his hands shooting a little humanitarian lightning bolt.

"Blizzards!" Vera drew close to Gus. "Heat waves..." She nestled closer and his alligator pants made independent moves again, scales glistening.

"How you gonna do all this?" asked Gus, stepping back from Vera, whose breath could bring down a B-29.

Ross Webster stepped between his sister and Gus, and moved his fingers lightly in the air. "Like everything else in the Twentieth century, Gus, You push buttons."

Gus let his yo-yo down, and contemplated the spinning rainbow.

I'm in control of the nex' move, he thought to himself, forgetting that only a half-hour before he'd been trying to escape the building in a ball-bearing chair.

He spun his yo-yo over his shoe tip, as the day seemed to fall back into place again, his big scheme still working, only now it was working on an even higher level. Go with it, he said to himself, everything is comin' into line.

He'd forgotten about his recent plans to crawl out the window and parachute into the company vegetation.

He could only see big money coming down.

My mind's *loose*, said Gus to himself. He relaxed, knowing he had a good run of dots here, the decimal point floating over to the hundreds, thousands, millions, hundreds of millions. He looked at his yo-yo spinning:

He saw himself living in a castle on a cliff above the ocean. Outside the castle was a limousine as long as a shopping mall. Stepping from it was Gus himself, in albino alligator pants, and dark glasses. Diamonds are flashing on his fingers, and a modest jewel has also been implanted into his right nostril.

". . . tell me more 'bout the weather," he said, looking at Vera.

6

"Smile," said Jimmy Olsen as he manned his camera. He stood in the office of the *Daily Planet*, his leg broken.

Standing before him, clad in holiday wear, were Mr. and Mrs. Maury Stokis, winners of the Bingo Jingo contest. They were indeed smiling, like a pair of hamsters.

"I can't believe it," said Mr. Stokis. "It's the first time I've ever won anything!"

Mrs. Stokis, feeling unusually hamsterish in all the excitement, put her head on her husband's shoulder. "You won my hand, Maury," she said, a dementedly sentimental smile on her face.

"Yeah sure," said Stokis, "but this is the first time I ever won anything valuable."

Jimmy Olsen hobbled around the office, knee cast bumping into things as he sought another angle from which to photograph the Jingo winners. Trying to ignore the situation in his office was Perry White, editor, smoking at his desk. The relentless Miss Henderson had him by the shirt sleeve. "Let's get a photo with you in it too, Mr. White."

"I haven't got time." White stabbed toward his desk with his cigar, pointing at a headline he was trying to write.

". . . and with the sombreros on . . ." Miss Henderson brought the gaudy oversize headgear down around the couple. They smiled moronically and struck a Latin motif, as Olsen clicked his camera.

"Now, Mr. White, you get in the picture, handing them their plane tickets."

"Why do I have to do this," whined White, throwing down his copy page.

Miss Henderson tugged him by the collar, into the picture, as she smiled at the Stokis's. "Mr. White is so happy for you folks."

"Yes, I am," said White, forcing a cheesy smile, as Miss Henderson twisted the knot in his tie.

"Smile!" said the lamebrained Jimmy Olsen.

"South America," said Mr. Stokis. "I can't believe my luck!"

Gus Gorman sat in conference with Ross and Vera Webster. His yo-yo was in his palm, in the off position, but it was still warm from humming. He listened as Ross Webster spoke: "Computers talk to other computers, don't they, Gus?"

Gus swiveled his head toward Vera, as she spoke: "Somehow," she said, "your twisted little mind should be able to figure out how to tap into the main computer at the Aerospace Center and reach Vulcan."

"Through the telephone-line terminal," said Gus. "Nothin' to it."

"Oh Bubba," squealed Vera, "think of the possibilities."

"What'd she call you?" asked Gus.

"She called me Bubba," said Ross Webster, uncomfortably. "When she was three years old she couldn't pronounce the word 'brother' and it came out 'bubba.' I've been forced to bear the name since." He looked at his sister. "Vera, if you don't stop calling me that I'll tear off your epaulets."

"I'm sorry, Ross." Vera appeared momentarily contrite, but it was not a feeling that came easily to her tyrannical nature; however, fearing her brother's wrath, she remained seated with her hands between her knees, in a manner of sisterly coyness which ill suited her, owing to the faint impression people always had, that she would look better with a mustache.

The door opened and Loreli Ambrosia entered, carrying a charred penguin. "Look what I brought you, honey," she said, going over to Webster.

Gus's yo-yo fell to the floor at the sight of Loreli; he could see her stepping out of his limo when he became a millionaire. He'd take her into his castle above the ocean and give her a penguin of his own.

Vera Webster followed Gus's gaze and gave him a dirty stare. "*She's* not his mama either," said Vera petulantly.

"Didn't think she was," said Gus quietly, as he continued to stare at Loreli's voluptuous profile, which caused his yo-yo to go up and down.

Parts of this lady I would like to walk-my-doggie on.

Ross Webster gestured with the charred penguin toward Loreli. "Gus, this is my Psychic Nutrition-ist."

Loreli stepped over to Gus. "You're cute."

What's she tryin' to put past me, wondered Gus, and sat down beside a coffee table, on which an oversize chess set was displayed. He moved the black knight, just to show her what was what. To his surprise, the board answered his move, pieces swiveling automatically around and checkmating him. He recovered his composure and gazed back up at her. "Jus' what does a Psychic Nutritionis' do?"

"I feed the ego," said Loreli, sweetly.

Have to get me a Psychic Nutritionis', thought Gus, after my first hundred million come down. Have her feed my ego three, four times a night.

"Here, Loreli," said Webster, "put my penguin in the desk."

Loreli took the burnt bird and opened Webster's desk drawer. While Loreli's hand was inside, Vera took the opportunity to ram her formidable hip against it, thereby pinching Loreli's fingers in the drawer. Loreli winced but made no sound as she couldn't let Ross know that his toad of a sister had scored a point. Webster, however, noticing Vera's eccentric hip-action, turned:

"What's going on here?"

Vera smiled, as Loreli waved her pinched finger in the air. "She's drying her nails."

Ross Webster, his overfed ego naturally misunderstanding, smiled at Loreli. "Always making yourself beautiful for me, aren't you?"

Loreli smiled pathetically, and Vera gloated triumphantly; Gus Gorman reminded himself never to hang his yo-yo or any other part of his anatomy in an open drawer when Vera Webster was around. He turned now, toward Ross Webster, who once again posed the question: "So, Gus, you can make Vulcan do what I want it to do? You didn't answer me, my friend."

Gus hesitated. He didn't much care for the tone in Ross Webster's voice, which implied that Gus Gorman was just a two-bit hustler who'd do anything for a buck. "Say, Mr. Webster, I'm not sure I like what I'm hearin' here 'bout my part of the action."

"Did you hear about that prison riot last week?" asked Webster, with a warm smile. "It seems the inmates were complaining about rats in their cells."

"'Bout this Vulcan, Mr. Webster, I figures I can go in there, punch a button, and come back out 'fore anybody knows what's happenin'." Gus gestured nonchalantly. "Type of thing a trained programmer can do, like that." He snapped his fingers, while visions of prison rats passed through his mind, great big ones carrying dinner menus featuring jailbird's toe for an appetizer. "So, in answer to your question, yessir, I can do it."

"When?" asked Webster.

Loreli interrupted. "Your first question should be *where*."

Ross Webster turned toward her, a look of surprise on his face. Then, seeing it was just gorgeous Loreli trying to be an executive, he gave her a patronizing smile. "Look dear, why don't you just go—"

"—and powder my brain." Loreli gave a pert little nod, and began to withdraw from the conference, but the sly glance she slipped Gus showed that she was not as dumb as everyone thought. Gus gave her a sly glance in return, which said that when he was rich he would take her to his castle and show her how his yo-yo worked underwater in a hot tub.

Now he turned authoritatively toward Webster. "Your Psychic Nutritionis' happen to be right, in this one case. You do need to figure out *where* you do this, if you don't want them to trace it back. So you punch it in from someplace nobody'd ever think of. Some rinky-dink operation with a Micky Mouse computer."

"Well," said Webster. "Webcoe has a hundred and twelve subsidiaries and every one of them is tied to our central computer system. How about . . . hmmmmm . . . someplace small . . ."

"Smallville, next," said the bus driver.

Gus stared out the window of the bus. At first, he'd been worried about Smallville law enforcement agencies but as he approached the outskirts of the city his apprehensions vanished. A couple of cops were assisting a road crew there, and they looked like they had number 2 gravel for brains.

Gus smiled through his tinted window as he rode by them.

They wouldn't recognize a computer crime if it happened in their own police station.

I'm doin' fine. Won't be no trouble here.

The bus entered the city and made its way to the dingy little terminal. Gus stood and took down his Vuitton suitcase, containing several tastefully made lizard shirts and a spare pair of crocodile pants. Humming to himself he made his way along the aisle and down the steps of the bus.

Gonna walk away with this town. Put it in my back pocket, zip it shut, and faaade.

Because there ain't nobody roun' here smart enough to stop me.

Gus stepped off the bus onto the sidewalk. A car door opened and struck him in the leg.

"Owch! Goddamn . . ."

"Oh," said an abashed Clark Kent, "I'm terribly sorry."

Gus limped off, muttering. He would normally

101

begin a lawsuit in a case like this, whereby permanent damage to the shinbone could be claimed.

However, under the presen' circumstances, I'll let it pass.

He walked on, shaking off the pain, and took a look around at the downtown environment. A nearby clothing store featuring menswear in the window attracted his eye; a closer examination revealed a green-and-white polyster leisure suit of the sort Gus wouldn't use to shine his Ferrari.

The dumbbell who'd just hit him in the leg had been wearing a similar model.

7

Clark Kent and Lana Lang motored out of Small-ville for a picnic in the country. Ricky Lang was with them, cuddling a small puppy in his arms, and the backseat was filled with blankets and a picnic basket. Ricky and the puppy played affectionately, and in the front seat Clark and Lana were having their own little game of puppyish play, their eyes meeting from time to time, for no reason.

"It's so strange to be back here," said Clark, "renewing old acquaintances."

"Anyone special?" asked Lana.

"Oh, for instance," said Kent, "that old farm-house up ahead. I used to play nearby it when I was a kid. Yes, that old farmhouse means a lot to me.''

Is he toying with me, wondered Lana, or is he just a sentimental booby?

"Tell you what," said Clark, "I know a little dirt road that runs right on by the farm. We can have a swell picnic there—with lots of memories.''

He turned down the dirt road, and followed it until they found a warm grassy spot, with a view of the farmhouse and of the big grainfield Clark Kent had run in as a boy. "That's a great place to play, Ricky,'' he said, pointing at the rows of waving wheat. "Almost like a jungle.''

Lana Lang spread the blankets and opened the picnic basket. An array of plastic containers came out. Ricky and his puppy bounced around happily. "Do they have picnics in Metropolis, Mr. Kent?''

"Not quite like this," said Clark, looking up at the sky and fields where he'd spent his boyhood wondering why it was he could leap over a corn silo in a single bound.

"Mom and I do this all the time," said Ricky. "Come on, Buster!" Ricky raced off, the puppy bounding along stupidly beside him, wagging his tail. In a moment, they'd disappeared into the grainfield, leaving Clark and Lana alone on the blanket.

"It's nice for Ricky," said Lana, opening the containers. "And even nicer when there's a man around. Which isn't often.''

Clark looked at the various containers. "There's a lot of choices here.''

"No, all the good ones are married." Lana unscrewed the lid on the thermos bottle.

"I meant all the choices here," said Kent, casting an eye over the containers. "Cole slaw, guacamole—this is some picnic." He dipped a fork in a container and sampled its contents. "And this pâté is marvelous," he said, smacking his lips.

"Pâté?" Lana leaned close to him, and peered into the container. "I didn't make any—oh Clark! That's Buster's dog food!"

In this way, Clark Kent had revealed himself again as someone not really of Earth, but as an alien for whom dog food and pâté were much the same. But Lana Lang could only conclude that he'd revealed himself again as a stupid dumbo. Yet the look in his face as he removed the fork from his mouth made her laugh, and his twitching little attempt to cover his embarrassment made her like him even more, and her laughter carried her against him.

Attempting nonchalance, Kent laughed too, as if he always ate dog food as a conversation starter.

"I haven't laughed like that—" Lana raised her head from his chest, where it had fallen. "—since I really can't remember when."

"Neither have I," said Kent, who would have eaten an entire case of Ken-L **Ration** if it meant being liked.

And yet something told him that his love-suit with this girl was hopeless, that other responsibilities, higher ones, would intervene at the crucial moment. He knew it was true, knew that his inescapable destiny was to fly faster than a speeding bullet.

But once again, some other part of him longed to be mortal, and know the simple unencumbered pleasures to be had in a mortal woman's arms.

Lana may have felt his conflict, for now she drew self-consciously away. "So...how much longer do you think you'll be in Smallville?"

"You know, I was just thinking, Lana, someone like you could do real well in Metropolis."

"Someone *like* me?" asked Lana, raising an eyebrow slightly.

Kent buried himself in some macaroni salad. Was it fair to lead Lana on? Can someone able to jump six thousand miles in the air ever expect to lead a normal married life?

"I suppose," said Lana, "I've got to face the fact that I'm not finding what I want in Smallville. But could I make it in Metropolis? I mean, what would I do when I got there?"

"Call me," said Clark, unable to stop himself from playing with her emotions. Did he have some sort of male-ego game going? Did he have to feel women were his for the asking, even though he'd sworn to avoid intimacy with them? It troubled him to think this was so, for it meant that Lana Lang didn't really matter—all that mattered was that the divine female form of Earth could be swayed toward him.

But Lana *is* special, said another voice inside

him. She's so like you, so modest, so unassuming. You're perfectly matched and you do care for her.

But why, asked the other voice, is it always *beautiful* women with whom you're so patient and kind?

Have you thought of that?

"Oh," said Lana, "I wouldn't want to call you. I mean, I *would* want to, but I wouldn't want to be a nuisance to you."

"Hey, you could never be a nuisance."

This is love talk, said Kent to himself. I'm at it again and I hardly know it, because it creeps up inside me. I'm under Earth's spell, as I must be if I'm to live my life here. But perhaps Lana will be the sensible one . . .

Lana moved toward him, touched his knee. "Clark, may I tell you something?" Her voice grew softer. "My oil pan is leaking."

A variety of confusing images played across Kent's brow, troubling him still more. A warm flush came over him, and he looked into her eyes.

She turned and pointed to her car. "See?"

A few dark drops fell steadily from the underside of the vehicle.

"May I help?" he asked.

Lana, I can lift this car with one finger, repair the crack in your oil pan with the molten power of my super-vision and have you rolling again in about three minutes.

Lana opened the trunk of her car. "No thanks. With all the trouble this car gives me, I started studying auto repair."

So saying, she slid under the car and began banging around with a wrench.

Kent could only stand beside her in admiration, of her tenacious application of latent talent, and the shape of her legs.

But while engrossed in this pleasant contemplation, Clark Kent found his mind slipping into a higher level. Danger, he realized, was threatening somewhere near.

Scanning the grainfield, he noticed a thresher had entered the rows, its great turning blades chopping at the slender stalks. And his superhearing brought him the insistent whine of a puppy, close to the thresher.

A flash of super-vision penetrated the grain, to the place where Ricky, in a fit of boyish abandon had knocked himself out on a stone. The whining puppy sat beside him, licking the child's forehead, as the thresher came closer and closer to turning them both into Wonder bread.

"I think," said Clark Kent, "I'll go and play with Ricky."

He moved quickly toward the fence that bordered the farm. Once behind it, his civilian clothes began to fall away, and the great rush began to fill his veins, the incomparable knowledge that he was Superman!

He zoomed into the air and circled the grainfield. A moment later he was diving toward the blades of the thresher.

The driver of this machine, a bored and possibly

dull-witted farmhand, was lazily dreaming of corn liquor and sex.

Naked damsels as featured on the calendars at the local garage came to him, bearing large jugs.

He put their jugs to his lips.

With a pleasant fantasy like this to occupy him up on the seat of the thresher, it was no wonder he was about to unknowingly thresh a boy and his dog.

He dreamt on, burped to himself, gave it a little more throttle, when suddenly—

—a gol-durned tornado!

The tornado was Superman. He gripped the whirling blades of the thresher and stopped them dead, which caused the driver to pitch forward and smack his head against the frame. "... say, what in hell you think you're doin'..."

Superman reached down into the grain and lifted Ricky and Buster, holding them up for the driver to see. The driver's mouth fell open and his cigarette dropped into his filthy overalls. "Holy-o-corncakes," was all he could say. It would have been a day without pay had he threshed a good hound dog and a boy. There'd a-been 'splanations to make, and he hated 'splanations like hell-fire.

"Th-thanks, mister," he stammered, rubbing the natural and unnatural bumps on his head, and tried to get his machine in gear again.

Superman, meanwhile, rose into the sky, Ricky and Buster in his arms.

"Superman?" asked Ricky.

"That's what they call me," said the Man of Steel.

He gave the frail youth a moment then, soaring with him, high into the firmament, showing the boy Earth's sublime form. At the same time, the grand musculature of his own form sent intense pulsations of power into Ricky, putting grace, elasticity, and physical prowess into the boy's frail anatomy, so that he could successfully defend against his cruel friends in future and in fact kick their ass if he so desired. All this happened in the space of an instant, as Ricky's cry of joy rang in the sky. And then they were back on Earth, beside Lana Lang's car.

She was just now crawling out, pretty knees foremost, perhaps to deliberately give Clark something to think about besides dog food pâté. But to her incredible surprise, it was not Clark but Superman who stood before her, with Ricky beside him.

"Ricky? Where . . . what . . ."

Superman indicated the cut on Ricky's forehead. "I'd put some iodine on that."

"Thank . . . you," said Lana, still dumbfounded at the sight before her, of godlike Superman in bright costume, the fabled Odysseus of the stars.

"Anytime," he said, keeping it low-keyed.

"I'm Lana Lang. This is Ricky."

"We've met," said Superman.

Lana turned, to introduce Clark Kent. "Clark?" She looked at Superman. "My friend is around here somewhere, I'll just look for—"

"I'm sorry," said Superman, in a kindly voice. "I'm in a real hurry." He turned to Ricky, whose body now contained a special vibration, to shape its muscle and increase its speed. "See you around, pal."

With a smile and a wave, he took off into the air. A supersonic *swoosh* sounded over the grainfield, and he was gone.

"We were flying!" Ricky jumped up and down. "In the sky!"

"But where did he find you? Did you get lost?"

"I was playing with—" Ricky looked around, calling. "Buster! Buster!"

The little dog's bark echoed from a nearby culvert, out of which Clark Kent was coming, the puppy in his arms. ".'I found him!"

Ricky ran over to Clark. "Mr. Kent! Superman was here!"

Lana joined them. "He really was!" Her face was flushed with excitement—and with something else Clark had seen in women's faces when Superman was around. A ridiculous feeling of jealousy passed through him. "Lana, I'm from Metropolis. I see Superman every day."

"Can you get me his autograph?" asked Ricky, still bouncing. Had someone taken notice, they might have seen that he was buoyant as a balloon, or else steel springs had somehow come into his calves.

Mild-mannered reporter Clark Kent (Christopher Reeve) who is in reality Superman is about to face his greatest challenge yet.

Reformed ne'er-do-well Gus Gorman (Richard Pryor) is a highly unusual genius who is finally given the opportunity to use his computer expertise.

Ross Webster (Robert Vaughn), Chairman of the Board of Webscoe Industries, who wants to one day rule the world, is named Humanitarian of the Year.

The two women in Ross Webster's life: his sister Vera (Annie Ross—top), and his girl friend Lorelei Ambrosia (Pamela Stephenson—bottom).

Superman saves Jimmy Olsen's (Marc McClure) life at a fire in a chemical plant.

Ross Webster makes Gus Gorman an offer he can't refuse.

Vera, Ross, Gus, and Lorelei contemplate an electronic map of the world as they discuss their plans for industrial world conquest.

(Bottom) Gus gains access to a remote computer of Webscoe Industries in Smallville by getting former-football hero, now nightwatchman, Brad Wilson (Gavan O'Herlihy), drunk.

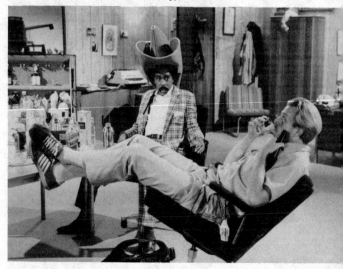

Meanwhile Clark is reunited with his former highschool sweetheart Lana Lang (Annette O'Toole) at the Smallville High School reunion of the class of '65. Later, on a picnic they continue to make up for lost time.

Disguised as a general from the Pentagon, Gus presents Superman with the synthetic Kryptonite to prevent him from interfering in any more of Ross's plans.

Using his heat vision, Superman welds the hole in the hull of an oil tanker, reversing the damage caused by the oil spill.

Hidden in a large cave at the base of the Grand Canyon, Ross views Gus's handiwork, the Ultimate Computer.

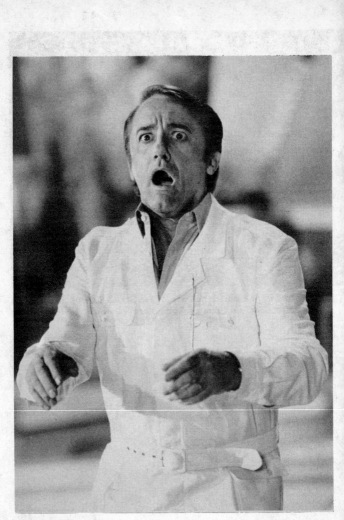

Ross is terrified when he realizes that he is now at the mercy of the out-of-control computer.

Weakened by the computer's Kryptonite ray, Superman is forced to find a different way of stopping it before it's too late.

Through their combined efforts, Superman and Gus are triumphant in the destruction of the Ultimate Computer, and they part company at a West Virginia coal mine.

8

When night fell on Smallville, a transformed Gus Gorman was climbing into a rented car; his wearing apparel appeared to be rented also, from the store window on main street, for he now wore a green-and-white polyester suit and looked, he thought, just like a Smallville geek.

Blendin' right in, he said to himself as he checked his reflection in the rearview mirror, and pulled out onto the road.

A few minutes' driving took him to the edge of town, and into the heart of an industrial park situated there, one of whose buildings was marked *Wheat King Farm Machinery/ A Webcoe Company*. It was in front of this building that he parked, and stepped out, briefcase in hand.

Blendin' and glidin', said Gus softly to himself, as he walked across the parking lot and up the front sidewalk to the door of Wheat King. There he located the night bell, and rang it.

A flashlight appeared in the corridor, and the night watchman's shadow came down it, footsteps echoing in the darkness. Were any of the local sports fans there, they might have found the rolling gait of the watchman familiar, for it was that of Brad Wilson, former golden boy, who'd lost his beer franchise and was now employed by Wheat King, owing to the kindness of the owner, Eddy Roebush. Roebush had been Wilson's tight end back in the past, and was frequently tight in the present, down at a Smallville gin mill called the Sportsman's Club. Many sportsmen had been clubbed there, with chairs or anything else that might be handy. Having shared a good many such occasions with Roebush, it was only natural that Wilson should come to him for employment. And so, only a few nights before, he'd begun work, with a solemn promise never to drink on the job. He staggered down the hallway now, seeing double.

After a few moments' fumbling he found the microphone gizmo that connected him to the threshold. He spoke through it gruffly. "Yeah, whattya want?"

"Buddy," said Gus, "we're in trouble."

"What?"

"Firs'," said Gus, "the supplier couldn't find the invoice. Then the order came up short. Then I missed the four-o'clock plane from Clevelan' and had to rent a car, and then I had a flat tire.''

''What're you talkin' about?'' asked Wilson, mind fuddled.

Gus leaned confidentially against the window glass. ''Talkin' 'bout your boss.''

''Mr. Roebush? Tight Eddy?''

''Rosebush, that's the guy! Say, he's gonna nail your yo-yo to the wall. This is a Special Order. He said he had to have it before—what's tomorrow?''

''I dunno, Tuesday, I think.''

''Tuesday? I got to get it all set up *tonight* before those big shots come here tomorrow for the meeting.''

''Well,'' said Wilson, ''I've got to see some ID.''

Gus opened his briefcase, and showed him a row of vodka bottles.

Sometime later they were sitting together at a desk, the bottles spread before them, half empty. Gus, in rocky shape, was shaking a cocktail for Brad. ''This one gonna be the one.'' He bent over Brad's glass and poured.

Wilson lifted the drink to his lips. ''S'not bad, s'very good . . .''

''Gonna name it after you.''

''You know what they ushta call me in high school?'' Wilson gestured, pouring part of the cocktail on his shirt. He was taking it slow, just drinking enough to feel mellow and relaxed. ''They ushta call me the Shmallville Flash.''

"Good name for a cocktail," said Gus, and shook up another one. "Here you go, Flash. You got an amazin' c'pacity, you know that?"

Wilson took the cocktail. "I jush drink t'be sosh'ble . . . coupla drinksh . . ."

"You never pass out?"

"Nope—" Brad closed his eyes. "—never." His head clunked down on the desk.

Gus leaned over, studying Wilson. "The Flash look flushed." He lifted Wilson's arm, and it dropped back down heavily. Gus reached over and extracted the ring of company keys from the unconscious watchman's belt.

"Now le's see here . . ." He studied the key ring, his own vision somewhat blurred; but Gus always had a ledge to stand on, no matter how drunk he got.

Conditionin'. Been trainin' since I was six.

He left the office and swayed along through the hallways of Wheat King. Turning a corner, an unexpected mirror greeted him, with an image of himself in the green-and-white polyester suit. He jumped back in horror. "That is terrifyingly ugly."

Be glad when this job is done an' I can get back into some sens'ble clothing . . .

With his share of the profits he'd be able to buy a pair of rhinoceros-horn shoes he'd seen.

Tips curl up.

Beautiful shoes.

Le's see, where am I?

He moved from door to door until he found the one he was looking for, marked *Computer Center.*

116

It housed, as he'd hoped, a rinky-dink computer. But it required two keys to activate it, key A and key B, to be inserted simultaneously.

He inserted key A and leaned over to add key B.

"... too much stretch ... gonna have to get the Flash ..."

He walked back out and down the hall, to the office where Brad Wilson slept.

"Hey, brother! Hey, Flash!" He shook the comatose Wilson, but the Flash was nowhere near consciousness, his mind buried deep.

"... god ... damn ..." Gus got Wilson under the armpits and lifted his dead weight upright; then he dragged him out of the office and down the hall.

Man feel like a cast-iron stove ...

... drag him along here, practically kill myself ...

Gus hauled Wilson into the computer room and propped him against console B, with the key in his fingers. Wilson, still unconscious, snored heavily and kept sliding out of position. Gus tied a yo-yo string to Wilson and with its aid kept the Flash upright. He dashed in front of his own console, let out some slack on the yo-yo string connected to Wilson and the night watchman pitched forward, key foremost, inserting it into console B just as Gus inserted his own key into console A.

The machine lit up and said hello.

"Ok," said Gus, "you and me gonna be friends ..." He began touching buttons, and the program came on. The buttons flew and computers sleeping far away woke up and they too said hello.

Gus wandered through, a hundred million yo-yo strings glowing beyond his fingertips. "...ok, believe I've got what I need to make some weather..."

As he hooked into what he thought was the Aerospace Program, another computer far away clicked on. It was housed inside a bank, and just outside that bank a man was withdrawing his plastic bank card from his pocket and walking toward the Instant Cash machine in the bank wall. He had exactly fifty bucks left in his account and was about to withdraw it in order to engage in one last bout of reckless spending before jumping off a bridge with a horse-weight tied to his ankle.

"...enter my code...push withdrawal..."

He stood, waiting for the bank's computer to run his card through and deliver his last fifty. After a few moments a thunk in the money drawer announced his cash had been released. As he opened the drawer and reached for it, another pack of fifties clunked down. And another and another.

"...son...of...a...bitch..." He scraped up the bundles quickly, stuffing them in every pocket, as more thunks sounded, bundle after bundle dropping down.

Back at Wheat King Computer Center, Gus shook his head, and corrected his error. His fingers flew again, dipping once more into the big brain and activating another distant computer.

At a later date, in a breakfast nook, a man will

open his morning mail and find a computerized charge his wife has apparently run up at the local department store, totaling $176,784.57. He will put a grapefruit in her face.

". . . tha's not the one either," said Gus to himself, fingers continuing to contact computers around the country and the globe, including one that controlled traffic on a street corner in another time zone, where pedestrians were waiting to cross and go to work.

The little red man in the stop light changed to a little green man, and people crossed, only to find halfway across the intersection that the little red man was back, holding up his hand.

". . . hey, whud's goin' on, mac . . ." A fist was raised at the computer-controlled little red man, and he turned green, then red, then punched himself in the head and disappeared.

On Gus's screen a series of interlocking corridors appeared, forming the three-dimensional pattern of a runway. He keyed on, taking off, and started to climb.

HELLO, said the computer screen. VULCAN WEATHER SATELLITE. CONFIRMED.

". . . 'bout goddamn time . . ." Gus's fingernails clicked quietly in the half-light of the Wheat King Computer Center. Beside him, Brad Wilson slept on, dreaming a curvaceous cheerleader clad only in cowboy boots was walking through the pickle-brine of his mind singing boom-a-lacka boom.

REQUEST COORDINATES, said the computer.

Gus typed fast, making certain memory chips

cooperate, thus causing certain gates to open and bridges to lift deep inside the circuitry.

"Not a bug anywhere," smiled Gus, yo-yo strings of high and low voltage flashing. A hundred signals ran through a gate, stopping just at the edge of Infinite Page Fault, and held steady.

VULCAN PROGRAM. EARTHSCAN. COMMAND.

"Damn straight, this is Commander Gorman on the key."

LONGITUDE 98 DEGREES

"...talkin' 'bout some weather..."

LATITUDE 175 DEGREES

"...gimme some lightnin' and a couple bars of thunder..."

LOCATION COLOMBIA, SOUTH AMERICA

From the belly of Vulcan, turning high above the Earth, a double beam of laser light flashed out, toward South America.

In a little South American village, nestled in the jungle, a peasant was leading a pair of donkeys. Seated on the donkeys was another pair of donkeys— Mr. and Mrs. Maury Stokis, Bingo Jingo winners, on their all-expenses-paid vacation. Tropical insects were stinging them and the donkey had earlier stepped on Mrs. Stokis's handbag, crushing her sunglasses.

"Isn't it a wonderful vacation, Maury," cooed Mrs. Stokis, as her beast of burden lumbered under her, lost in his own thoughts.

El burro es muy perezoso, the burro said to himself.

And twitched his ears.

For it felt like rain.

Which meant he wouldn't have to carry this fat gringos around no more.

"Look, Maury," said Mrs. Stokis, "there's a native wedding!"

"Whoa," said Mr. Stokis. "Stop. Halt." He called to the Indian leading the beasts. "Hey, Pancho, put on the brakes, will you? Thanks, thanks, that's a good boy."

The ninety-year-old patriarch held the animals steady, while Mr. and Mrs. Stokis climbed down, clutching their cameras. "It's so wonderfully quaint," sighed Mrs. Stokis, as the wedding party began coming out of the church; she swung her weighty camera into position, for one of her special on-the-tilt slides. "I think I have a classic study here, Maury..."

The donkey's ears continued to twitch. There was something very strange in the air today. Something high up in the sky...

"Take two pictures of it," said Mr. Stokis, who liked to act as director on shots like these, with your touch of native in the background. He'd show all his wife's slides later in the year and feel himself tilting off his chair for days afterward.

"... and get one of that bush there, it looks authentic..." Mr. Stokis leaned against his donkey and waited for his wife to collect the shot.

...go home, take some Mylanta, have a few drinks. It should be a nice evening.

He was at peace with himself, for none of it was costing him a dime. "Ain't that somethin', Pancho? Me and the wife winning a trip like this?"

The elderly donkey-master looked at Mr. Stokis, and looked at the sky.

"...of course, I shouldn't have eaten that chicken-in-a-coconut. Now that I see how they raise those birds." Mr. Stokis gestured toward a pile of trash, on which he assumed all South American poultry was raised. "You been in this racket long, pal?" He looked at the patriarch holding the reins, but the old man did not answer. His eyes were on the sky.

The sky was filling with clouds the likes of which he had never in ninety years seen.

Dark clouds of ancient menace.

...*Santa María*...

"...found myself comin' apart after eatin' that chicken...so we found this little restaurant that serves your American food..."

...*ai caramba*...

"Somebody said Ava Gardner usta hang out there, whattya think?" Mr. Stokis put his sombrero back and looked at the sky. "A touch of rain, Pancho? One of your seasonal showers?"

...*caramba*...

The sky opened. A torrent of water fell into Mr. Stokis's somebrero, soaking him down. In a moment's time he was lost behind a sheet of water thick as Niagra Falls.

...one of your tropical flashes...be over in a second...

"Maury, where are you? Maury, where...are..."

His wife's voice was lost. The village street was a cascading torrent. On all sides people were rushing for shelter, as the whirlwind of water rushed down.

9

"... meteorologists baffled by the tornado and torrential rainstorms that struck the country of Colombia this afternoon, threatening to destroy the nation's entire coffee crop for the next five years..."

"... a spokesman for the Department of Meteorology at Cal Tech here said this was and I quote, 'the most awesome display of natural forces since Noah's Ark.' He added that the storm's pattern seems to defy all known laws of weather systems..."

Images of destruction flashed on the television screen, of a country in ruin. The Humanitarian of the Year smiled.

"I tried to reason with them—" Ross Webster

shook his head, at a country so stupid as to defy a leader of his stature in the business community. He climbed into his ski togs, a simple man of humble tastes, whose citation in the Rolls of Humanitarianism read "... for leading the world through modest example..."

He stepped out onto the terrace of his penthouse, which had been turned into a private ski resort. Twenty-seven tons of snow blanketed the massive space, some of which had been raised to provide him a practice slope. He walked to the slope now, and was elevated up it in a mechanical chair, above the simple but charming après-ski chalet he'd constructed on the roof. "... I spoke to them honestly... I told them my feelings about their country..."

He attached his skis and gripped his poles. Below, the city was suffering a heat wave. Up here Ross Webster enjoyed a little modest exercise. He pushed off and glided down the slope. It was a gentle one and brought him down in a spray of snow, beside Loreli Ambrosia, who was tanning herself in front of a reflector.

As cold snow fell on her, she leapt up squealing, "Oh, I'll get you for that, you big silly!" She rolled a snowball and threw it at him, Webster laughing at the girlish way his Psychic Nutritionist pitched. Loreli didn't care; she had shares of preferred stock in Webcoe now, which had done wonders for her own psyche. Goofing on the roof with Webster was a small price to pay, she felt, as she lobbed another playful snowball at him.

Nearby, goosebumps of loathing ran up Vera Webster's back as she contemplated her brother and that squealing, stupid little gold digger. Vera called for one of the maintenance men, told him to pour a few gallons of water on the ski slope.

"But that'll turn it into a sheet of ice. Anybody gets on that they'll go sailing—" The maintenance man looked toward the distant edge of the penthouse terrace.

"Don't ask questions," said Vera, for it would soon be Loreli's turn to take a little ski trip, twenty stories to the street below.

"Ok," said the maintenance man, trudging off for the hose. He'd give 'em water, up the gizenta. They want water...

He connected the hose.

...they'll get water.

Vera, meanwhile, had joined Ross and Loreli at the TV set, where further broadcasts of the Colombian holocaust continued. Vera looked at the people floating away on their houses and gave a girlish giggle. "Ross, do you realize what we've done?"

"The coffee trade is ours," said Webster, nodding. "Every time a drunk tries to sober up, he'll be drinking a Webster blend."

Vera's beady eyes started to glow. Her expression of everyday avarice became one of exalted greed. "Why stop at coffee? A cup of coffee gets the world off to work in the morning, but what *keeps* the world working?"

"Diet soda?" squeaked Loreli cutely.

"You silly little twit," sneered Vera. She hoped that her brother could see the difference between her keen mind and Loreli's pathetic mentality.

Loreli smiled to herself. Webcoe stock had risen ten points today . . .

Ross Webster was staring at Vera. What *did* keep the world working? he asked himself. As the world's leading humanitarian he'd always felt it was exploitation of the labor force and creative accounting that kept things going. But it occurred to him now that there was a raw substance beneath these things. "Vera . . . you mean . . ." He slapped his head with his hand. "The magnitude of this!"

"Today coffee," said Vera.

"Tomorrow oil!" Ross Webster came out of his chair.

They want water, said the maintenance man, turning on the hose above the ski slope, I give 'em water. He watched it flow down the grade and shook his head as it turned instantly to ice.

"Oil!" shouted Webster, staring into the sky, fabulous visions of wealth and power before him.

"Oil?" asked Loreli, rubbing some on herself to promote a healthy tan.

"You're such a hedonistic little slut," said Vera, who did not tan, owing to a tendency toward pink blotches. "Ross," she said, turning back toward her brother, "if our computer programmer could press the right buttons—"

Ross Webster gripped the back of an après-ski chair. "All the oil! All the tankers! All the pumps!

I'll control it all!'' He bowed his head, in modesty. The world would be licking his toes.

He turned toward the TV screen, to enjoy more of the reportage from Colombia, a country that'd know better next time than to give a great humanitarian any shit.

Yes, there was some footage of a family clinging to a floating door...

...people wading mud up to their neck...

Superman flying by...

"Superman?"

SUPERMAN!

The Man of Steel flew with cosmic grace, fist clenched before him, into the heart of the demonic storm.

I was born for this, he thought, as he hurtled down through the churning maelstrom. Here was a worthy opponent, a giant of power, inhuman and violent beyond imagining, the wind itself.

It tore at his speeding form, as it had torn houses, autos, entire streets and great buildings from the ground; but he plunged through the tornado's grip, as if it were a summer breeze.

He found its whirling base, where mad frenzy ruled; debris of every kind rained against his body, stone walls, iron girders, flying machinery, but he brushed them aside as if they were gnats. His mighty hand reached, gripped the tornado's tail, and yanked.

The whirlwind turned inside out, its force spent in a single second.

He scattered the cloud remnants, and calm prevailed.

"Super Hombre!" called the people below, hanging from flagpoles, crawling from mine shafts, staggering stupefied through their villages.

But Superman's work was not done. He flew to the coffee plantations, where the torrents of water still flowed. His swift form descended, cape streaming; he landed in the rivers of mud and water and summoned the fires of Kryptonic force that coursed in his veins. Twin beams of star-flame shot from his eyes, attacking the water, drying it in an instant, steam rising up as from the jungle at dawn. The land was cleared and the coffee beans saved.

"Super Gringo!" called the grateful workers, tossing their hats in the air. Now their monthly salaries of $2.45 would be paid! Now they would not starve.

Superman sped to the next plantation and the next, drying their anguish like the tears of a child; for variation he sucked up all the water flooding one plantation and spit it into a nearby crater, turning it into a lovely lake.

"El Super Comerciante!" cried a local entrepreneur who, owning the crater and all the land adjacent to it, could now open an overpriced resort.

Only Ross Webster was unhappy. Staring at his TV, he slumped down into a ski chair. "No, no, no . . ." He wrung his hands in grief. "It was the perfect plan! Foolproof!"

"But we were the fools," said Vera, blood pressure pounding, pink blotches of emotion turning her the color of a medium-rare hamburger.

"He ruined it! That lousy do-gooder, he ruined it." Webster shook his fist at the TV screen, where Superman stood smiling, hands on hips, staring out at the world.

"Don't cry, Bubba," said Vera.

"Don't call me Bubba." Ross shook his head, defeat weighing heavily on him.

Loreli Ambrosia sought to solace him with a mug of steaming mulled wine. She handed it to him, first removing the steaming bag of spices and dropping it into Vera's hand.

"AIEEEEEEE!" Vera shot up, flailing her arm.

Ross Webster swiveled around angrily.

"Vera's practicing her karate," said Loreli.

Vera might well have succeeded in the sport, for her knees were like porcelain doorknobs, and once, in a rage, she had bitten through her own watch strap. Now she would have settled for Loreli's heart, but Ross Webster intervened with more important problems.

"Superman'll stick his nose in my oil scheme too," whined Webster. "I've got to get rid of him. I've got to!"

"But how?" asked Vera.

The door of the penthouse opened and Gus Gorman walked through. Webster snapped at him. "Did you see what Superman did? Why didn't you consider *that*?"

"Hey, don't go blamin' me," said Gus. "Superman's a tough dude." Gus backed away, out of Webster's shouting range. He didn't need that kind of scene.

He faded in behind the ski slope. ". . . not my fault things didn't work out. I did what I was supposed to do. But that's always been the way, even in school. Teacher accidentally back into an open switchblade, who took the rap? Gus Gorman . . ."

He climbed up to the top of the ski slope and looked around, as Ross and Vera carried on below, about Superman:

"Someone ought to be able to stop that big self-righteous goon," said Webster.

"How?" asked Vera. "Shoot him? You know about him and bullets. Not to mention knives, tanks, bombs."

"Kryptonite," said Loreli sweetly, patting tanning oil on her cheeks.

"What?" snarled Webster.

"Or Kryptonham . . . or is it Kryptonheimer? I forget what you call it," said Loreli, reverting to her stupid-blonde role, a blend of insouciance and lethargy which carefully disguised her corporate ambitions; one day she'd have controlling interest of Webcoe. "Anyway, whatever it's called, it's the only stuff that can hurt Superman."

"How would you know?" hissed Vera.

"I know a lot of things," said Loreli airily.

"So I understand from the graffiti I've seen," said Vera, whose own form had been depicted on

132

the Webcoe lavatory wall, intimately embracing the nose of a crudely drawn fireplug.

"Wait a minute," said Ross Webster, interrupting the tasteless exchange. "She's right! Kryptonite. I read about it in an interview with Superman, except—" A crestfallen look came over his face. "—there isn't any more. The only chunk that ever landed on Earth disappeared a couple of years ago."

"Where did it come from?" asked Vera.

"The planet Superman came from. Krypton."

"Where is Krypton?"

Gus Gorman answered from the top of the ski slope. "It blew up. Superman got shipped to Earth when he was a baby." Gus poked a ski pole down and lifted a tablecloth up on the end of it; he fastened the cloth around his neck like a cape. "Man been flyin' aroun' ever since." He extended his arms in imitation.

Vera started to warn Gus about the ski slope, but Webster diverted her attention. "When a planet explodes, debris is left floating in space. We just have to find out where in heaven Krypton was. Then good old Gus here contacts the Vulcan satellite—"

Gus, attaching skis to his boots, looked down at Webster. "Just hold on a minute. I've been doin' some thinkin'."

"Good," said Webster, "that's what I keep you for."

"*That's* what I've been thinkin' 'bout. How you've been keepin' me. I'm not gettin' enough outa this gig. Haven't even been able to buy my rhinoc'ros boots.''

"Gus," said Webster, "if there's one thing I hate, it's greed."

"Greed?" Gus gestured with a ski pole. "Lemme tell you somethin' 'bout greeeeeeeeeeeeeeeeeeed..."

Gus was sailing down the iced ski slope, skis racing over the frozen surface.

Hey, what's goin' on here? I 'pear to be pickin' up some speed...

A moment later he was shooting off the end of the slope and through the air; he glided over tables, chairs, and the terrace wall. Tablecloth waving behind him, he began falling twenty stories toward the ground.

I fear I have made my firs' and las' ski jump, brother.

Windows be flashin' by me...

...goddamn tablecloth in my way here, can't get no balance...

He thrashed with his poles, straightening his cape, and looked straight down.

I'm sinkin' a whole lot quicker than I should wish to.

Windows continued fluttering by him as he fell. Few inside the Webcoe building even saw him, so fast did he drop by. Owing to the velocity of his fall, Gus's perceptions were heightened and he had certain spiritual insights:

...fine-lookin' secretary bendin' over that desk...

...'nother one crossin' a tough pair of legs...

Too bad I won't be roun' at coffee-break time.

But I'm going to be breaking into 220 billion pieces, time I hit the ground.

Probably go right through the sidewalk...

...end up in the subway somewheres.

Helluva way to go, ain't it?

...man with my po-tential.

He stared at the traffic below, each detail of it growing rapidly larger.

One item began to stand out more clearly, directly in his trajectory. It was a glass roof, sloping toward the street. He thrashed his ski poles, straightened his cape again, and angled onto it.

His skis slid over it and he sailed off the end, his next glide taking him at the optimum angle to the pave. He sped along it, sparks flying off the bottom of his skis, and came to a stop in traffic, as people gathered around.

"Holy god, you see that!"

"...guy came down on them skis..."

Gus lifted a ski pole, trying to appear nonchalant. "Practicin'. I'm an O-lympic jumper." He moved forward, clacking along the pave.

A close one, brother. Jump like that you got to bend your knees *just* right.

10

"What're you working on?" asked Gus's colleague in the Webcoe Data Processing Center.

"Just spacin' out," said Gus, fingers gliding over his computer keyboard.

LOCATE AND SEARCH X GALAXY AT 3500 LIGHT YEARS

"It's coffee-break time," said the colleague.

"You go on ahead," said Gus. "I'll catch up."

ANALYZE COMPONENT ELEMENTS OF KRYPTONITE PARTICLES

Gus's screen went blank momentarily, as his instructions were processed. Then the machine answered:

INSTRUCTIONS RECEIVED

"Well, I guess I'll go then," said the colleague,

inserting a pen in his nerd-pouch. "Don't work too hard, Gus. It's not *you*."

"...hear you talkin'..."

SCANNING X GALAXY

The Vulcan satellite, obeying Gus's command, pointed itself toward that region in space where a mighty planet had once been and was no more. There, green Kryptonite fragments floated, ancient pieces in a puzzle never to be put back together.

A door in Vulcan slid open and its laser beam shot out, into Galaxy X. Its brilliant beam searched and found a glowing fragment of the lost planet.

The beam touched it gently all over, caressing it in space as the fragment wandered in eccentric orbit.

KRYPTONITE. AN INTENSE FUSION OF:

PLUTONIUM...15.08%

TANTALUM...18.06%

XENON...27.71%

PROMETHIUM...24.02%

The laser beam penetrated to the innermost secret of the fragment, and paused. Gus's computer screen hummed faintly, as he waited for the rest of the analysis.

DIALIUM...10.48%

MERCURY...4.08%

The computer readout remained steady, and then the final line was added:

UNKNOWN...0.57%

"Unknown?" Gus looked at the screen. "What kinda jive is that? What am I going to do if *you* don't know what it is?"

Gus stared at his screen. Nothing more was forthcoming.

He looked down at his desk, and did some thinking.

Ross the Boss would not go for 0.57% unknown.

Ross the Boss must have it *all*.

Idly, Gus's eyes traced the label of a package of cigarettes lying on his desk.

NICOTINE 8%, TAR 5%

Gus returned to his screen, erased UNKNOWN 0.57% and inserted TAR 0.57%.

"Man won't be smokin' this mixture, so I don't see how it matter much." He punched the printout, received a written analysis of Kryptonite, including 0.57% tar, and carried it down the hall to the offices of Research and Development.

A white-coated mad scientist looked up as Gus entered. Gus smiled and handed him the Kryptonite analysis. "The Boss wants this, to go."

Mr. Maury Stokis, arm broken, leg in a cast up to his hip, looked around him angrily as he pushed Mrs. Stokis's wheelchair through the hallway of the *Daily Planet*. Mrs. Stokis herself had both legs in a cast, and wore a neck brace as well. Both of them, as will be remembered, had nearly lost their ass in a windstorm while enjoying the Bingo Jingo prize vacation.

"Where is he?" shouted Mrs. Stokis, staring straight ahead, head locked in position by the brace; only her lips, eyes, and jowls moved. "He'll pay for this! Get your wallet out, Mr. Editor!"

Mr. Stokis matched his wife's bellow with a gesture of his cradled arm. "... fractured by a flying brick," he said matter-of-factly to a passing copy boy, as if presenting early evidence in the lawsuit. He hobbled along the hallway, the memory of the storm's fury still very much with him; at night in dreams he was seeing chicken feathers and empanadas sailing by him. Naturally, his lawyer was including irreparable mental damage in the suit.

"... we had fifteen more dancing lessons comin' to us," said Mrs. Stokis to no one in particular, referring to the Autumn Harvest Dance Program she and Mr. Stokis belonged to in Metropolis, at a local dance studio noted for swindling middle-aged couples into paying exorbitant prices for learning the tango. Mrs. Stokis could not dance now, owing to the amount of plaster she was carrying around and the neck brace which would prevent her from snapping her head dramatically in the tango turn.

She would sue the *Daily Planet* for the lost dance lessons, and more, much more. Her native shawl had been ripped from her in the storm, along with her Indian-embroidered blouse and brassiere. Personal humiliation had resulted as she'd found herself clinging, half naked, to the side of a public building while a number of men rolled by in the wind, apparently jeering.

Her lawyer had explained it all to her.

"... and I'm a modest woman," she was saying now, eyes straight ahead, neck upright. Coming toward her was Miss Henderson from the Circulation Department.

"Get your wallet out!" repeated Mrs. Stokis, gaze fixed on Miss Henderson.

"Please, Mr. and Mrs. Stokis, it isn't the *Daily Planet*'s fault—" Henderson put a sympathetic hand on Mrs. Stokis's arm.

"Don't touch me," said Mrs. Stokis bitterly, thinking of her lost tango, her broken legs and neck, and of the sombrero Miss Henderson had given her, the draw string of which had nearly strangled her when the hat was blown off her head by a two-hundred-mile-an-hour wind.

"Mr. Stokis," said Miss Henderson, turning to Stokis, "*you* know it wasn't our fault."

"I know I got hit by a flyin' brick." Stokis lifted his cradled arm again, pointing the elbow at Miss Henderson. He flapped it. "Now, if you'll step aside—"

He wheeled the dour-faced Mrs. Stokis through the doorway of Perry White's office.

"What the hell is this?" asked White, turning around, recognizing neither Mr. Stokis nor his wife.

Mrs. Stokis angrily wriggled her naked toes, which peeked out from the ends of her casts. "Bingo Jingo!" Her jowls jumped up and down. "The contest!"

Mr. Stokis stepped out from behind the wheelchair, cast thumping. "Mr. Editor, my wife's neck's been stuck in one position all the way from Colombia. She eats through a bent straw, and you are goin' to be breathing through one by the time the court gets through with you.'' Stokis nodded confidently, elbow still working the air like a paddle.

Miss Henderson stepped up to White's desk. ''They were caught in that terrible Colombian storm, while on our Jingo vacation.''

''You and your Jingo,'' muttered White, then went immediately on the offensive, for lots of people sued him, all the time. ''It wasn't the *Daily Planet*'s fault,'' he snarled at Stokis. ''It was an Act of God.''

Mrs. Stokis stared fiercely forward, eyeballs trying to roll sideways toward White. ''We *happened* to be in a church.''

''That's right,'' said Mr. Stokis. ''So don't go pullin' your Act of God with *us*. We're taxpayin' Presbyterians.''

Mr. Maury Stokis closed his eyes, the scene painfully imprinted on him, of the church suddenly disappearing behind a sheet of rain and Mrs. Stokis being lifted in the air by her sombrero; then chicken feathers, doors, donkey harnesses, and a great many other things had gone flying by, including Mrs. Stokis's Indian-embroidered bra.

''...never been so outraged and humiliated...'' Mrs. Stokis tried to gesture with her chin, inching it forward over the cushioned metal brace.

''You haven't got a leg to stand on,'' snapped White.

''You're goddamn right I don't,'' countered Mr. Stokis, thumping his cast forward. ''Nor Mildred.

The poor woman's confined in front of her canary cage all day. Oh, you'll pay, don't worry."

Beyond the windows of Perry White's office, Clark Kent looked up momentarily from his typewriter, but the spectacle of Mr. and Mrs. Stokis hardly registered on him. He was typing a story, one with great meaning for him.

... old relationships suddenly seem the same as ever ... the prettiest girl in the school is still the prettiest girl ...

His telephone rang, and the prettiest girl herself was on the line:

"Clark," said Lana Lang, seated in her kitchen in Smallville far away. "Ricky got overexcited and told all the kids that Superman is coming to visit him for his birthday next Wednesday."

Beside her stood the forlorn youth, whose ecstatic flight with Superman was a thousand dreams come true; he wanted more, wanted the sky for his birthday, and thought it couldn't hurt to ask. And his mother had seemed very eager to call Mr. Kent.

"... ok, I know I was wrong," said Lana, "but when Wednesday comes and Superman's not there, well, you know how cruel kids can be."

Clark knew. How often in childhood he'd been hit in the head with a stone, or jeered at by supposed friends. And strong as he was, Child of Steel that he'd been, it'd still hurt; the stone may have bounced off but the feeling of rejection remained. "In this case, Lana," he said, "I think I can speak for Superman. I mean, I'm pretty close to him, you know.'' He paused, wondering if it was right, then plunged ahead. ''Superman will be there on Wednesday.''

Lana spun happily on her kitchen stool. ''Well, he's going to get the best home-cooked meal he's had in a long time. You tell Superman we think he's wonderful.'' She paused, wondering if it was right, then plunged ahead. ''But Clark—you're the best,'' she said softly.

11

The mad scientist employed by Webcoe carried a tray from his laboratory out into the waiting room, where Gus Gorman sat. The scientist placed the tray on the table in front of Gus. Upon the tray was a glowing green substance with a surface resembling lava. "There you are. I can't imagine what you want with it—" He waited for Gus to give him a hint. The substance, as far as he could tell, was about as useless as frog manure.

But Gus was eyeing the rocklike substance warily. Even though born of the laboratory, it seemed alien, like something he might find coursing through his periodic dream of being lost in a subway tunnel, with this thing coming at him out of the dark.

Gus touched it gingerly, his nervous fingers almost dropping it. The mad scientist turned back toward his lab; he'd made many strange things for Ross Webster and sometimes it was better not to know what their use would be; this was obviously one of those times. In any case, he could now return to his research work on a nutritionless loaf of whole wheat bread made entirely out of recycled paper bags.

The lab door closed. Gus Gorman stood alone with the Kryptonite. "...some bad-lookin' stuff..." He shook his head, palmed the substance, and walked out of the Research Department. Unlike the mad scientist, he knew the purpose of the substance, and it did not make him feel good to think about bringing down Superman.

Superman was alright, had cool boots too, bright red.

"...but anybody ask me, I'm only followin' orders. I'm just one of the employees." His yo-yo, a walnut executive model, spun toward the floor. He walked-the-doggie with it, down the hall, as Webcoe personnel watched, plastic heads turning in their cubicles. Gus's Day Glo shirt fluttered and his alligator pants rippled. Yo-yo humming, he walked on by. "...jus' another face in the crowd, that's all. Jus' like all the other folks at Webcoe..."

Superman streaked across the farm belts of America, evoking cries of wonder from those farmers below who saw him, and creating moments of extreme paranoia and confusion in the already troubled minds of air traffic controllers from state to state.

His mission was not superhuman, nor did it challenge his greatness. It did show what a good guy he was, for he was on the way to Ricky Lang's birthday party. But perhaps it was not just Ricky he was going for...

He descended over Smallville, red cape streaming like the tail of a comet. Lana had told Clark Kent to have Superman meet her on the corner of Main Street in the middle of town; from there, she said, they'd take Ricky shopping for a present. Now, as Superman dropped down over Main Street, he saw the entire town out, with all its citizens and dignitaries, including Mayor Edward (Honest Ed) Fogarty. Mayor Ed, on seeing Superman in descent, took off his hat and waved it, the signal for the Smallville High School Marching Band to begin playing, nearly in tune.

Superman turned immediately upward, shocked by the shouts, the cheers, the banners, the cacophonous blaring of the band, which had placed next-to-last in a six-state musical contest only the month before.

High above the tinkling of the glockenspiel and the braying of the trumpets, Superman turned in the air. Self-preservation told him to depart at once, that at best he'd only make an ass of himself below. But his super-vision, scanning the crowd, found the eager face of Ricky Lang and, beside him, the nervous countenance of Ricky's mother, with the whole town on her back. If Superman didn't come back from the sky, she'd be humiliated.

He sped downward again, and landed beside her on the guest platform, to thunderous applause.

"... I really wasn't expecting all this," he said beneath the tumult.

"I'm sorry," said Lana. "People got carried away when they heard—"

Mayor Ed Fogarty was clearing his throat at the microphone. "Superman," he said, turning toward the Man of Steel, "we all know you're not looking for honors and awards—"

Mayor Ed Fogarty was not looking for honors either. Having recently been indicted by the grand jury in a price-fixing scandal, and with much to hide as regards certain construction contracts he'd recently awarded, Mayor Honest Ed Fogarty sought only to draw attention away from himself, and onto anyone else. "—but when I heard that you were coming to see your pal Ricky, I realized this was our chance to say thank you. First, for putting out the Lake Chanooga Fire. Second, for saving little Ricky from a threshing machine, and finally for the thousands upon thousands of things you have done for Americans everywhere. In my own small way, I try to emulate your honest, knightly service to humanity, and I'm sure everyone here today in their own way does the same. You have already won the key to our hearts, Superman, so may I present you with—" He picked up a presentation box. "—the key to our city."

This cumbersome and useless object was presented

to Superman along with a little gift from the
Ladies Auxillary—a spiral-bound edition of their
cookbook, whose recipes went back to the Revolu-
tion and had sped countless Smallvillians into high
blood pressure, gout, and early baldness.

"Thank you," said Superman, and held the
objects up to be photographed by the crowd. As
the flashbulbs popped, Superman turned to Lana
and gave her a reassuring smile. *It's alright*, his
eyes seemed to say. *I'm happy to be here*.

". . . having some difficulty locally," Mayor
Fogarty was saying to Superman from the other
side, quietly. "I'm sure you remember my father,
George Virtue Fogarty, who used to bowl with
Clark Kent's father . . . know you have a close
relationship with Clark . . . we helped send him to
college . . . some local muckrakers trying to ruin
the good name of Fogarty, and I thought you
might . . ."

The mayor's importuning was interrupted by the
sudden blaring music of yet another marching
band, broadcast through the loudspeakers attached
to a khaki-colored jeep with *U.S. Army* stenciled
on the side. At the wheel, in WAC uniform, was
Vera Webster. Riding behind her, in the uniform of
a five-star general, was Gus Gorman.

Clad in white helmet, foulard ascot and jodh-
purs, and bearing a swagger stick under his arm,
Gus rose as the jeep skidded to a halt in front of
the reviewing stand. Vera turned toward the crowd:
"TEN-HUT!"

Conditioned by years of war movies, the good

citizens of Smallville snapped to attention, including Mayor Fogarty, who'd served with valor during World War II, lending money at 200% interest to fellow soldiers stationed in New Jersey.

Gus stepped from his jeep and strode up onto the platform. The crowd watched in silence as he took the center of the stage and turned to address them:

"Lissen up! I'm here direc' from the Pentagon, to tell you that God has given us the greatest goddamn gift in the world: chemicals!"

The crowd knew then: Gus was speaking of Superman's recent saving of the Eastern seaboard from chemical fallout.

Gus, on stage, continued to rant in militaristic fashion.

"If we don't protect our chemicals, it's our ass!" He stared down at the High School Marching Band, where the baton twirlers were blushing.

"And democracy's ass!" he continued, cutting the air with his swagger stick. "And the free world's ass!" He turned toward the Ladies Auxillary. "You want to be able to go to Church on Sunday and rest your well-fed butts on molded plastic, don't you? How come we got such high-grade plastic? 'Cause we got the bes' chemicals on the face of the Earth!"

"*Get to the point,*" hissed Vera, standing stiffly at attention before him.

In real life, Gus's military career had been spent as a private in Alaska, trying to unfreeze the engine block of the truck he was supposed to drive; promotion never came nor did the truck ever start; his request for a Purple Heart owing to a frozen nostril was not granted and he was told by his commanding officer he was lucky not to be in the stockade, permanently. Thus, his desire to continue at length today, in the uniform and style of a five-star general:

"You want the President of the United States signin' peace treaties and then the pen breaks and spills ink all over his pants in front of other world leaders because we got shabby chemicals?"

"... *get to the citation, you moron* ..." snarled Vera, under her breath.

"Now las' week," continued Gus, "this great nation almost bit the bullet, 'cause of poison hot acid rainin' down on our backyard barbecue. Wasn't anything we in the military could do about it—we were busy protectin' our borders at the time. And just when it looked like curtains, and I don't mean the Iron Curtain, I mean *all* the curtains—"

"...*the token of appreciation* ..." muttered Vera, yanking at Gus's pants leg.

"... along come Superman and saved our bacon. Superman, we got a little token of appreciation here for you—" Gus snapped his fingers and Vera handed Gus a small wooden box. Gus turned toward Superman. "It's your government's way of sayin', right on, Soup', you doin' real good."

Gus handed the wooden box to Superman. The Man of Steel opened it and found himself staring down at a mounted piece of glowing green Kryptonite. The ugly burnt shape spoke to him with a dark tongue hidden inside it somewhere, a tongue of evil and doom. It staggered him as its dark radiance poured forth; but the open air dissipated it, for he recovered his composure a moment later. "Thanks, General. It's . . . swell."

Gus was staring at Superman, expecting him to fall ill, or at least to faint, for the substance was nearly perfect, perfect enough he thought, to give Superman *some* grief. But Superman's gaze seemed steady as ever, and it made Gus uncomfortable.

"Well . . . uh . . . I've got no time to stick around for the corn-on-the-cob and the square dancing or whatever it is you people do. We got some marchin' to catch up on, and then some top-secret runnin' around followed by lunch . . ." Gus backed nervously away from Superman, and then hurried down the steps to his jeep, where Vera was already waiting. She turned to the crowd: "At ease! Siddown!"

Her remarkable resemblance to Stalin, accentuated by her military uniform, caused the crowd to obey her once again. They sat, and she roared off in a cloud of dust, through the town square, as Superman discreetly closed the wooden box and pushed it away from himself.

12

"What?" shouted Ross Webster through the telephone. "He didn't die? I ask you to kill Superman and you're telling me you couldn't even do that one single thing!"

"...ran into some *unknowns*," said Gus, from a phonebooth outside Smallville.

"What the hell are you talking about?"

"Talkin' 'bout zero point fifty-seven percent."

But 0.57% is not a great deal in any mixture . . .

Superman sat with Lana Lang, his powerful form and brilliant costume seemingly out of place in the small cozy living room. Usually his gracious manner, his simple elegance, allowed him to be at home anywhere, but he was obviously restless this night, eyes darting away from the photo album Lana had dragged out, his gaze toward the dark window instead.

Lana rose from the couch. "I have to check on Ricky—" She walked to the boy's bedroom, and found him fast asleep, in dreams of flight. She closed his door and returned to Superman's side. "He was asleep before his head hit the pillow." She smiled at her guest. "Well, this was only the biggest day of his life. I don't know how to thank you."

Superman glanced around the living room; its walls seemed foreign and faintly threatening, as if the atmosphere of the little house were pressing in on him.

What nonsense, he said to himself. Nothing can hurt me. I'm invulnerable.

"You'll have some coffee, won't you?" asked Lana. She rose and went toward the kitchen. She too was nervous, but not as nervous as she should be perhaps, with the most fabulous creature on Earth in her living room. But there was something so familiar about him, as if she'd known him for years . . .

Superman let his super-vision run aimlessly over the room; he picked up tiny details, of no consequence. What was he searching for? Why was he so uneasy?

The telephone rang, and he sprang from his chair; the room itself seemed to draw back, so forceful was his move. Then, hearing Lana answering the phone in the kitchen, he could only prowl the room like a caged animal, and finally, in frustration, he sat back down on the sofa.

Suddenly, Lana came from the kitchen and spoke almost in a single breath: "Superman, there's been an accident on the old River Bridge. A trailer truck jackknifed and crashed through the barrier rail! It's hanging off the side of the bridge and the driver is still in the cab!"

Superman stared at her, but didn't move. "There's no rush," he said, and Lana stopped, surprised.

"But the bridge—"

"Don't I always get there in time?" He smiled and patted the sofa. "Come on, relax."

Lana told herself that Superman must certainly know his own business. Her insistence that he rush out was probably very naive. Someone as fast as he was didn't have to hurry, of course.

His arm came up around her.

My, she thought, he certainly *is* fast.

"It's hard to believe," he said, "a great-looking girl like you with no one breaking down her door for a date."

She looked at him. Those blue eyes which had seemed so deep and endlessly serene this afternoon on the grandstand now had another cast to them, their expression much closer to the surface. "I just can't figure it," he said, his hand closing tighter on her.

"Listen, are you *sure* you shouldn't do something about the bridge?" Why did she suddenly fear him? Would his affection crush her to pieces? He was, after all, a god, wasn't he? He wasn't really *human*. And those eyes were so strange all of a sudden, so abstracted and cold, and they seemed no longer blue, but rather, green.

Green as that thing they gave him today, she thought, and her nervous fear suddenly increased. "The bridge," she repeated. "Shouldn't you—"

"The bridge?" He looked at her, his expression vague now. Then the green cast left his eyes, and the bright blue returned, whirling up from within. "Yes, I'd better get going!"

He rushed from the house and leapt into the sky. The great moment of acceleration came, but he feared momentarily that he would fall, that he would wake from a dream and discover he was plunging wingless to his death.

Get hold of yourself, he said, curling his fist into a pile driver of densely packed atomic force. The clouds drew back, and thunder sounded over Smallville as he flashed through the sky.

He soared to the bridge site and swooped down toward it, in time to see a pair of divers emerging from the water, a half-drowned truck driver in their grasp, and the truck itself gone, to the bottom of the river.

He landed beside the emergency crew. "What can I do to help?"

"Not much of anything now," said the sheriff, looking down at the truck driver, who was sputtering water and coming to his senses.

"...she jackknifed on me..." He looked around,

toward the gaping hole in the bridge. "Did I lose 'er?"

"You lost 'er," said the sheriff.

"The boss'll make me eat this load," said the driver. "I'll be drivin' without pay for the nex' ten months."

The sheriff looked at Superman. "If you'd come a minute earlier, you coulda saved his truck. Well—" He sighed, no ax to grind with Superman, who'd probably had some other rescue operation elsewhere. "—you lose some, you win some."

"...I lost 'er," said the truck driver, lying in a puddle of water and mud, shaking his head. "...eight tons of produce...lettuce...tomatoes..."

"Relax now, take it easy."

"...some cauliflower, I dunno, bunch of other things..." He babbled on, coughing water, as Superman looked on in dismay. The Man of Steel turned then, abruptly, and flew off.

He flew through the night sky, across the time zones of the ocean, flying aimlessly, trying to sort out his thoughts. The great sea heaved beneath him, its power like his own—vast, incalculable, mysterious in origin and destiny. He flew, and feasted his eyes on its tempestuous nature, and he exalted, to know that he was the same—unpredictable and to be turned by no man's hand.

I rule this planet, he said to himself as he flew.

His eyes were green as the green sea, and tossed by storms of emotion that came and went in violent waves. Never had he ever celebrated his own greatness, but always played it down.

But why?

Why not strike a pose Earth could not forget? Why not act like the master of might he was?

His green blazing eyes were matched by another green—that of his uniform, whose deep blues and reds had changed to the sinister shade of Kryptonite itself.

He crossed the Atlantic, and came at dawn to Italy, his course still aimless, but his body enjoying the exhilaration of that very aimlessness. A man of steel may do as he wishes. A god goes where he pleases, for no reason.

On the ground below, in a street in Pisa, a man of much simpler designs was just opening his sidewalk souvenir shop. Within it were rows of cheap plastic Towers of Pisa, each of them leaning.

"Hello, my friends," he said to the plastic items, and wondered how many the tourists would carry off today. He prayed the number would be many, for his aged mother needed a new hearing aid, and his wife wanted a motor scooter.

"Getta you souvenir towers here," he said, calling to the street, where early-morning tourists were already out, stumbling around.

"...take home a nice-a Tower, leaning justa-the-way the real one does..." He pointed at the venerated object, the source of his lifetime's income.

Racing toward it was a bluish-green dot in the sky.

Tourists whirled with their cameras, to get a shot of—SUPERMAN!

"What is he doing here?"

"Saving somebody, you can be sure of that."

He was in fact flying full tilt toward the Tower, a strange grin on his face. With a single push he straightened the long-leaning building into the upright position. It creaked and groaned, but stayed that way, and the skyline itself seemed distorted to those used to the Tower's tottering ways.

"...*mamma mia...*" moaned the souvenir salesman, his entire stock rendered more worthless than it already was—his leaning plastic towers no longer replicas of the original.

The greenish-blue form of Superman sped by him, in a whirlwind.

"*Super-cretino!*" shouted the salesman, waving his fist at the sky. "*Stronzo!*" Hysterically, the salesman turned back to his souvenir stand and, uttering another cry, began to smash his wares off the shelf. "...junka...justa buncha junka..." He sat down and wept, amidst his broken plastic towers, as the tourists and citizens continued to gape at the perfectly erect landmark of Pisa.

13

The next few days were the strangest in Superman's life. In Melbourne he performed a little tap dance, an idiotic grin on his face, and precipitated an earthquake. In England, above the moors, where an International Girl Guide Jamboree was being held, he did some skywriting, filling the blue dome of heaven with gigantic and obscene graffiti.

In Greece, at the opening of the Olympic Games, the final runner received the torch and raced with it up the pyramid of steps. The flame, preserved unbroken for decades, had recently traveled for seven days over 970 miles; now the supreme moment had come, the passing of the flame onto the Ceremonial Pedestal. As the runner bent over with the torch to light it, Superman, the world's greatest athlete, appeared and blew out the torch. The runner, confused and upset, had to turn around, run back down the steps and get his torch relit.

These, and other insane acts of abandon, caused the world to wonder: What has happened to Superman?

"I'll tell you what's happened to him," said Ross Webster, addressing his colleagues at the conference table. "The Kryptonite is working. Ok, it didn't kill him, but it's turned him into a selfish, ornery, malicious, half-crazed being. In other words—"

"He's a normal person," said Vera.

"That's right," said Webster. "And now that Superman's out of the Nice Guy business—"

"We can get to work on that oil," said Vera.

In the adjacent conference room, Loreli Ambrosia sat with her reading matter for the day. She'd just underlined a passage in Kant's *Critique of Pure Reason,* and had now picked up her second volume, Sartre's *Being and Nothingness*.

Anyone who has ever looked at either of these books is aware that the result, for most people, is a feeling of inferiority and deep depression. The intricacy of thought in a single paragraph of Kant or Sartre can actually induce seasickness; several pages of it make you feel as if ants were crawling all over you.

How, then, can Loreli Ambrosia read these volumes?

The voice of Ross Webster came to her from the adjoining hallway; she quickly slipped the heavy tomes into her makeup kit and assumed an attitude of hedonistic lethargy.

Ross Webster entered, followed by Vera and Gus.

"Hi, honey," said Loreli, "am I in your way?"

"No, stick around," said Webster. "You might learn something."

In the center of the room was an illuminated map, showing all the oceans of the world. Miniature images of oil tankers were scattered around these bodies of glowing water. "Every oil tanker in the world is controlled, totally, by computer. Computers tell them where to go, how much oil to take on, where to deliver it."

"They've got no captains?" asked Gus, who once thought of going to sea himself, with a blonde on a surfboard, and later in a proud little boat filled with tradition and five tons of marijuana; he abandoned this plan when his contact was found with a decorative bullet hole in his forehead.

"Yes," answered Webster, "they have captains, but they take their orders from computers."

"And you," said Vera, pointing at Gus, "will command the tankers to sail toward a fifty-mile area in the middle of the Atlantic Ocean."

"And do what?"

"And do nothing," said Webster. "Just float there."

"Then how are the different countries going to get their oil?"

"You catch on fast, old buddy," said Ross

Webster. He turned toward his sister. "Tell him about the pumps."

Vera clicked a switch, the conference-room fireplace split in half, flames and all, and two illuminated panels slid out. They formed an electronic map of the United States. Miniature oil derricks blipped electronically, simulating a pumping action. "Every oil pump in America is run by computers," said Vera, turning to Gus. "You'll command the pumps to stop pumping."

"And then shut down the pipelines," said Ross Webster.

Gus nodded his head. "These are high stakes." He looked at the Websters, who'd told him his share of the profits would come at Christmas, in the form of a bonus. He wondered if they were jiving him.

"I want you," said Ross Webster, "to program one special command into all these systems. Tell them the orders are *irreversible,* so it'll be impossible for anybody to switch them back. Can you do that, pal?"

Gus drew himself up, tightened the buckle on his belt, and addressed Ross Webster. "You're gettin' what you want all the time. When do I get a taste?"

"I should think a taste of freedom is enough, don't you? Or would you prefer jail?"

Gus picked a bit of lint off his tastefully tailored neon shirt. "Don't lay that jail number on me no more. You need me out here doin' stuff for you more than you need me sittin' in jail doin' nothin' for nobody.''

Ross Webster, being a humanitarian business-man, knew that occasionally you must allow your employees to rise a bit, before you tear them to pieces, break their will, and finally fire them without notice. ''What do you want?''

Gus immediately emptied the contents of his pockets on Webster's conference table—matchbooks, paper napkins, envelopes, scrap paper.

Webster looked down at the pile of crumpled effluvia. He looked at Gus. ''You need a waste-basket?''

''These are plans,'' said Gus. ''Blueprints.''

''For what?''

''A computer,'' said Loreli, drawing near. Then, seeing that she'd revealed herself as something other than a twit, drew back. ''Or it could be a hair dryer . . .''

''We've already got computers,'' said Ross Web-ster. ''The biggest, most expensive ones in the country.''

''Not like this one you don't,'' said Gus. ''No-body in the world has got one like it because it doesn't exist yet. We have to build it.''

''You designed it?''

''In my spare time. It's a stone killer-diller get-down-get-it-on twice-on-Sunday giant computer.''

The strings in Gus's head were lighting up at the thought of it. He'd been putting it together for months, yo-yos spinning, gates and bridges lifting, messages flying. Ross Webster gazed at him now, intrigued.

"What will it do?"

"Everything."

"What will it get me?"

"Anything."

"Tell me more," said Ross Webster, smiling genially.

14

Out in the oil fields, the rigs were running, booming night and day. The hearty drillers shouted, laughed, punched each other in the face at lunch, and resumed work a half-hour later, eyes blackened. They were tough, they were making big money, and expected to keep on making big money. If people they didn't like came around, they'd back over them with a truck. Nothing could interfere with *their* workday. How surprised they were when, all at once, their rigs stopped running.

At the site of a desert pipeline, two employees were crouched over the pipe, wondering what was going on. "...not a trickle comin' outa the goddamn thing..."

They looked at each other, and looked at their Land Rover. They looked at the pipe and they looked at the vast and desolate plain of the desert. "...they'll blame it on us, shore as hell..."

"Well, le's go back to town and git drunk."

"Alright, might's well."

They climbed in their Land Rover and drove off. When they got to town, the lines at every gas station were two miles long.

PROCEED LATITUDE 241, LONGITUDE 73. AWAIT FURTHER ORDERS.

Out on the high seas, the oil tankers converged in the fifty-square-mile area, and wondered what they were doing there, floating around, looking at each other?

The computers clicked, repeating the message:

PROCEED LATITUDE 241, LONGITUDE 73

"That's the middle of the Atlantic Ocean," said one renegade captain. "And I'm not taking my ship out there to just sit, no matter what any damn computer says. We're suppose to go to Metropolis and we're *going* to Metropolis."

Vera Webster, staring at the illuminated map, glowered at the blip representing this ship. "What is this one doing in the lower right-hand corner?"

"It's a tanker!" shouted an upset Ross Webster. "And it's going the wrong way!"

Loreli Ambrosia removed her eye pads and rose lazily from her couch in the office. Her arms came gently around Webster's neck. "How many shares in Webcoe is it worth to you, for me to stop him?"

"Miss," shouted the police sergeant through his bullhorn, "can you hear me? Don't jump!"

In the crown of the Statue of Liberty, a young woman sat, preparing to jump. Her long hair tossed in the wind, her legs dangled over the side of the crown.

It was Loreli.

The wind rippled her skirt as she sat in her precarious and provocative position. The policemen below, with binoculars trained on her legs, felt she had everything to live for.

Racing up the stairs toward her were other policemen, intent upon rescue.

Racing through the sky, out of his mind, was Superman.

He'd been causing trouble around the world. Recently his picture'd been on the cover of *Time* with the banner

GOODNESS AT THE CROSSROADS

And now he circled the Statue of Liberty, eyeing Loreli, who seemed about to kill herself.

Force of habit, or perhaps something else, caused him to dive toward her rippling skirt, and land, directly beside her on the crown.

"I thought you'd never come," breathed Loreli with a sigh.

"Don't expect me to save you," said Superman

coolly. "I don't do that sort of thing anymore. If you want to jump, go ahead."

She uncoiled from the crown's edge and rose sinuously toward him. The sunset lit her from behind, or lit her behind if you will. In any case, her magnificent body was outlined clearly before Superman.

The Man of Steel felt a faint tremor pass through his mighty frame, as if a bolt had popped somewhere. His eyes were blazing green, like a twisted emperor's jade.

Loreli stretched a little, and touched his uniform. "Don't let me keep you from anything."

"I'm in no rush," he said, the wind blowing his hair around, except for the iron spit-curl on his forehead. "What did you have in mind?"

"Lots of things..." Loreli lowered her eyes demurely, if such an attitude is possible while standing on the edge of a statue three hundred feet above the sea, with a squad of policemen rushing up the stairs toward you bearing nets and ropes.

"Lots of things?" asked Superman. "Tell me about them."

"I'll *show* you. Back at my place. If you'll do me one little favor." She rubbed herself against him like a cat.

"Ok, what is it?" Superman lifted his chin to the sunset. "You want a ride?"

"I get airsick. You wouldn't like that."

"No, I wouldn't," said Superman, whose uniform had frequently been soiled by nervous survivors of some disaster at which he'd assisted; he'd made light of people throwing up in his cape, but no more. This was a different Superman. "If you don't want a ride, what do you want?"

"It isn't much. You see, there's this little boat. Well, not so little, really. And it's not going where it's supposed to go—"

Superman listened, nodded, and sped off, as the policemen jumped out onto Liberty's crown and rescued Loreli, holding her firmly in their grip so she shouldn't accidentally fall off the crown or down the stairs. "Oh, thank you, officers," she said, walking between them. "I don't know what came over me."

"Some guy stand you up, honey?" asked the kind police sergeant. "He musta been a real joik. Come on, we'll go have coffee and you can talk about it."

She quickly explained to them she was no longer suicidal, that it'd only been a silly whim. They were hard-bitten policemen, but seemed to understand.

"Maybe, though, I should still give her a body search, Sarge. She might be carryin' a concealed weapon."

"No, Mulligan, that won't be necessary. I'll take the young lady home in my cruiser. Come along, miss—"

While Loreli was being gently conveyed just a short distance to her place, Superman was covering hundreds of nautical miles, a wild glint in his eye. The Atlantic was below, glistening green at sunset, its whitecaps tossing, and once again its raw power was the mirror of his own. He gave an awesome cry and dove, to where an oil tanker toiled in the troubled mirror.

"Hey," shouted the watch, "here comes Superman to give us a hand!"

The deckhands saluted him, and waved their hats, then ran to the rail as Superman dove at the hull.

"What's he doin'?"

"Holy Jesus!"

The ship's alarm sounded, and the merchant seamen ran crazily fore and aft, for the hull of their ship had just been torn open by a grip of steel, and their cargo of oil was spilling out.

"He's nuts! He's sunk the ship!"

"Super-fruit! You super sonofabitch!" They raged at him, but he was already gone, into the darkening sky.

Loreli's "place" was actually the Webcoe penthouse; she lived in the ski chalet constructed there, with a view that rivaled the Swiss Alps. Coming into that view at the moment was Superman, like a glowing green fragment growing larger and more distinct.

He landed upon the terrace, and Loreli opened the chalet door. She was clad in figure-hugging thermal underwear. A fireplace burned within. "Care for a little après-ski?" she asked, as he walked toward her. Stepping across the threshold, he saw the bedclothes had been turned down.

* * *

Elsewhere, in another bed, Vera Webster sat reading, in a nightgown resembling a prisoner's outfit in the Gulag Archipelago. Her bedchamber was spartan, and in fact the mattress was horsehair and hard as a brick.

She was reading a book entitled *Advanced Computer Technology*. Like Loreli's reading matter, this book was the sort that made the mind itch, but Vera was clearly engrossed. Her lips moved slightly as she read. "... if that moron Gus Gorman can understand this stuff, so can I..."

Fierce determination was fixed to her brow like a miner's lamp. She dared the next paragraph to confuse her; it yielded to her penetrating mind. As will be remembered, Vera had gained a certain amount of scientific exposure in childhood, having been exposed from the waist up on her brother's electronic project board while he made her hair stand on end.

Now her fingers snapped the pages of advanced technology, and she read on through the night, the frizz ends of her Joseph Stalin coiffure faintly tingling.

15

Across the nation, gas station signs said *½ tank to a customer.*

Americans, always ready to bear such burdens, buckled down patiently in lines a mile long at every station.

"C'mon, move it, you joik-off! Move ahead!"

"... I'm movin', keep your shirt on ..."

Patiently, quietly, they inched forward; radiators boiled over, some exploded, engines caught fire, but the good people of America took it lightheartedly.

"I'm gonna ram it up your ass sideways is what I'm gonna do, you piece of gunk!"

"Yeah, you and who else?"

"Me and the six guys ridin' with me, that's who—"

Fenders were crushed, grillwork dented, teeth knocked out. At Joe's Diner, connected to a gas station, Joe shook his head, as waiting drivers slammed in for coffee and some of Joe's rock-hard doughnuts. "I seen shortages," said Joe, "but nuttin' like this." He clunked a doughnut on a plate, and poured a cup of his famous brew, which tasted like brake fluid. "...here y'go...alrigh', who's next..."

"Two of them doughnuts an' a coffee," said Gus Gorman, sliding onto a stool at the counter. His Ferrari was outside, forty-fifth in line.

Joe clunked down the doughnuts, looked out the window at the long, winding line, and shook his head again. "Somebody's behind this. You can't tell me there's no oil."

"Seem to be some in this coffee," said Gus. "You think I could pour it in my tank?"

"...who's next...yeah whaddya wan'...there's always somebody gettin' rich off crap like this," said Joe, moving down the counter. "And it's always the little guy who suffers."

Gus looked around him, at all the people he'd brought to grief, folks just like himself trying to get from point A to point B with some loose change left over.

What have I done to these people? he asked himself.

And what for?

He looked at his Ferrari, forty-fourth in line.

For a lousy sports car already been in the garage fifteen times?

For a pair of rhinoc'ros boots?

Must be somethin' wrong with me somewhere.

". . . turn on the tube, Joe," said a truck driver.

Behind the counter, Joe clicked the TV set, and a distorted picture came on. ". . . *Coast Guard spokesman said today that choppy seas ought to contain the oil spill for at least two weeks before it reaches the Nantucket Current. After that, it's just a question of which part of the East Coast gets the brunt of the spill . . .*"

"There's yer oil," said Joe, angrily clicking the set off.

The diner door opened and an hysterical woman ran in, clutching her golf cap. "Help! Somebody help! My husband's just been beaten up! Call the police! Call an ambulance . . ."

A man came in behind her, a handkerchief to his face. "It's alright, Dottie, they only . . . broke my nose . . ."

Joe shook his head again, and looked at Gus Gorman. "That's the third one today. And at night, it's worse . . ."

Definitely somethin' wrong with me, thought Gus.

"Cheer up, Gus," said Ross Webster. "I have good news for you. Your computer is being built as we speak."

"Yeah? How's she look?"

"It's state-of-the-art technology, Gus. We are

talking unlimited power. We are talking get-down-hot-cha-daddy-o whatever you called it.''

Ross Webster strode happily back and forth in his office, counting his gains. But then a frown slowly crossed his face, as he considered the other side of the coin: ''A machine this powerful is going to make powerful enemies. People who will want to destroy it.''

''Nobody is going to mess with my machine,'' said Gus, rising beside Webster. ''I'll . . . I'll . . .'' The yo-yos in his mind revolved. He looked at Webster. ''I'll build in a counterpunch! Anything attacks it gets counterattacked. And wiped out!''

''Any opponent?''

''All you got to do is find their weak spot.'' Gus began scribbling on Webster's blotter. ''You bet on my machine in any fight you name, you gonna win your bet.''

Gus's great natural engineering mind, balanced as a spinning yo-yo, whirred on through the details. The yo-yo gave light and led the way once more down Computer Corridor, as Ross Webster watched on, delighted that he had such an idiot savant on the payroll.

In a Smallville kitchen, Lana Lang was on the phone. ''No, I cannot go out with you tonight. No, I'm busy tomorrow night too.''

In a Smallville bar, on the other end of the connection, Brad Wilson smiled at his puffy reflection in the bar mirror; he was remarkably confident with women, considering none would have anything to do with him. "You're busy? Doing what?"

"I'll think of something," said Lana.

"You'd better start appreciating me," said Wilson. "What else do you have in Smallville?"

Lana hung up on him and Brad Wilson stared at the phone. It was inconceivable to him that a woman would hang up while talking to him. "...bad connection...punch some operator in the mouth..." He punched the coin box and dialed again. Women were putty in his hands.

"...*you've got the wrong number,*" *said Lana.* "*And please stop calling me.*"

She hung up again, and Brad Wilson let the receiver slip idly from his fingers. It dangled from its cord as he walked toward the bar. A neighborhood drunk, hunched over his ale, turned a bleary gaze toward Wilson. "D'ja score, pal?"

"Sure," said Wilson. "I always score."

"Thash right," said his companion, steadying himself on his stool, which he'd noticed had a tendency to tip sideways and spill him down to shoe level. "The good ol' end run..." He swiveled off the end of his stool, and wobbled slightly before regaining his equilibrium. "I'm blockin' for you, buddy," he said, and proceeded forward, into the arms of a coat rack, which illegally clipped him and then tackled him to the floor. "...there'sh a marker down on the field..." he muttered, thrashing amongst the coats.

The Smallville Flash helped him to his feet, and they staggered together toward the door, as did so many other Smallvillians that night, going slowly crazy from boredom in their good old hometown.

Except for Lana Lang, who couldn't take it any longer.

She dialed the offices of the *Daily Planet* in Metropolis. When she got no answer from the desk of Clark Kent, she went a step further: "Smallville Airport? What flights do you have to Metropolis tomorrow?"

Of course people go crazy in Metropolis too, and next evening they were finding their way to their own therapeutic barrooms. Among them, remarkably enough, was Superman.

The Man of Steel, never known to take more than a glass of wine at dinner and perhaps a fine brandy at its conclusion, sat in the Metropolis Lounge drinking boilermakers like a common bum.

His uniform had gone from dark green to black, and glowed like the costume of a vampire, filled with sinister intent. The look on his face was menacing and the only customers near him were those too drunk to move. Everyone else in the bar had given him a wide berth, including the bartender.

"Gimme another one," barked Superman, and knocked it back as soon as it was set in front of him. It took a great deal of Earth booze to intoxicate a Kryptonian, but he was getting there, a mean and stupid expression on his face. Certainly, if the man beside him did not have his own eyes closed in the peanut dish, he would have moved away.

Superman looked at his own peanut dish. He picked up a handful of peanuts and fired them at the row of bottles behind the bar. They landed like machine-gun bullets, shattering the bottles and the mirror.

Superman laughed, then caught sight of himself in the mirror; his once-noble face was fiendishly twisted. Angry at the image before him, he shot forth twin rays of heat from his eyes and melted the mirror, his image vanishing with it.

"He's washed up," said a woman standing in the doorway.

"Nobody'll ever trust that creep again," said someone else beside her.

"What're you looking at?" Superman leapt off his stool and the doorway cleared. He walked toward it, black cape swinging with menace.

He stepped into the street, and found himself looking into the faces of Lana and Ricky Lane.

"Superman!" cried the boy, overjoyed at the sight of his hero.

"Be careful, kid," said a bystander, one among many who had gathered to watch the spectacle of Superman's degeneracy.

Superman stared at Ricky, and walked on, as if this boy had never been sheltered in his arms, or meant a thing to him.

"Superman!" cried Ricky, following him. "It's me, Ricky! Ricky from Smallville!"

"Don't go near him, son," said a voice in the crowd. "He's dangerous."

"Superman," said Ricky, his voice breaking, "tell them you won't hurt anybody!"

Superman turned, and for a moment there seemed to be a flicker of understanding in his eyes. But the moment passed and he continued down the street, the crowd parting before him.

Lana Lang laid a hand on Ricky's shoulder. "Ricky, he's changed."

"No," said the boy. "He must be—must be sick!" He broke away from his mother and continued running after Superman. "Superman, please get better!"

Again the Man of Steel hesitated, and turned; but again the wolflike expression returned to his face, merciless and cold, as if he'd never flown with this child, had never given him strength and guidance. There were only strangers around him, mocking and hostile.

"You can hear me, can't you, Superman?" called Ricky, following up the avenue.

"He's not listening to you, Ricky," said Lana.

"Yes, he is! He's got super–hearing. I know you're going to be alright, Superman! You're just in a slump. You'll be great again. You can do it . . ."

The boy's eyes filled with tears, but the eyes of Superman were glowing coals of unrelatedness, the eyes of a bird of prey. He leapt into the air, and soared away, leaving a terrified and awestruck crowd below.

16

...you're just in a slump. You'll be great again...

Ricky's voice followed Superman, echoing in his tortured mind. He shuddered at the sound of it, and seemed to remember other times, of goodness and service.

...great again...great...

He shrugged in flight, shrugged off the voice. Goodness was illusion in a world not one's own.

He flew blindly, his gaze finally attracted to a landscape as grim as the state of his own soul. Strewn everywhere were twisted piles of metal, where small fires burned. He landed, in an automobile graveyard. On all sides were rust, corrosion, and debris.

...great...you'll be great again...

The boy's echo made him wince, and he cried out, his cry like that of a slain bull. It pierced the auto graveyard, startling the workers, who fled from their machines.

Superman stood alone, surrounded by heaps of steel, car bodies mashed and flattened. Smoke drifted through the air and wrapped itself around him, as if to welcome him. His body felt like lead, and his mind like the tangled scraps of iron piled on every side. As if veiled in smoke, his thoughts would not come clear, and he stumbled across the graveyard, its ugliness transfixing him.

Then a peculiar thing happened:

Emerging from the body of Superman was the form of Clark Kent, who appeared first as a faintly luminous figure but grew slowly more dense until he stood facing Superman with equal corporal weight.

Superman stared, startled; a portion of his power, he well understood, had just been taken from him, and had shaped itself into the form of this four-eyed oaf.

"I'm no hallucination," said Clark Kent, staring back.

"We'll see about that," snarled Superman, whose power, though halved, was still substantial.

"Give up," said Clark Kent.

"Like hell I will," answered Superman.

Clark Kent, Superman—these are just names for the raw kinetic energy of Krypton, a planetary power at war with itself. That it could divide into equal halves, like night and day, was only one of its brilliant possibilities. It could, as well, destroy itself.

One half, Superman in black—the shadowy nature of things Kryptonic; the other half, Clark Kent, embodying something quite different, the positive sun of that world: across the galaxy, fate had hurled this dual entity, and Earth had claimed it, adding its own touch to the mixture, and upsetting the balance.

"You always were an annoying creep," said Superman, taking a step toward Kent, whose faintly superior air now filled Superman with rage. He shot his fist out, striking Kent a blow which sent the mild-mannered reporter stumbling backward against a pile of axles, which collapsed around him. He rose slowly, obviously shaken, but Superman's own shock had been as great, for the jaw he'd struck had felt like something harder than iron—and he recognized the dynamic force of Krypton, facing him now, its molecular density great as his own.

Clark Kent came toward him. "I can give as good as I get. Are you willing to risk it?"

"Try me," said Superman, spitting defiance.

Clark Kent charged, head down, and butted Superman with such force the jaded hero flew straight back, and fell, into an acid vat. Chunks of metal protruded from it, like the arms of its devouring spirit; the mixture closed around him, bubbling and steaming, seeking to remove the flesh from his bones. It seemed instead to act merely as a hot tub, relaxing Superman's muscles. He sprang from it with new force, and blew a stream of the searing substance at Kent. It splashed all over Kent, burning his jacket off, but leaving his skin unharmed, as if the acid were no stronger than liniment. He had little time to enjoy the rub, for Superman clubbed him with a chrome bumper.

"I never did like you," hissed Superman. "You always got on my nerves."

Kent's rejoinder was a flying tackle, which carried both him and Superman onto a conveyor belt. They grappled on it as it moved them along, belt creaking, rollers grinding. Superman, hatred rising, heaved Kent off, into a pit, where cars were stacked, flattened like cardboard. Superman activated the controls of the hydraulic presser and sought to flatten Kent.

The iron press descended, tons of force landing on the reporter. He pushed against it, as if it were a Nautilus machine, suitable for increasing chest muscles. He pressed it up, threw it off him, and came out flexing his pectorals. A moment later he was hurling tires at Superman, which dropped around Superman like horseshoes, holding him fast.

Superman flexed his own muscles and split through them, and they fought on, with cranes and giant magnets, with wheel rims tossed like Frisbees. Car parts became hideous clubs in a primeval battle. The graveyard sounded with clanging metal and savage cries. If the spirits of Krypton were watching on, their sadness must have been supreme, to see their child of the stars battling himself in an insane rage, Superman trying to feed Clark Kent through a metal shredder.

The teeth of the machine split and broke over Kent's supernatural body, unable to chew it, the machine losing its own teeth instead. Superman, his gaze still clouded in madness, his only desire to kill, leapt on Kent again and they rolled, over and over in the graveyard, each trying to bury the other.

"Give up!" cried Kent, trying to choke his shadow-self, grappling in the dust with it; the eyes that glared up at him were like the evil memory of a race departed. This was Krypton, its wars, its villainly.

How can I suppress such force, Kent wondered to himself, his own mind halved, his own clarity less, his own hold no greater than his opponent's.

He called upon his aged father, the departed spirit who'd guided him through good and evil many times.

Was that spirit near? Can one planet call another, or memory speak? Kent saw, instead of a burning graveyard, a single candleflame burning in himself.

If the father's spirit was anywhere, it was there, in his heart. The flame flickered brightly, but then disappeared behind a cloud of smoke, the graveyard of Superman's evil soul. Clark Kent held his stranglehold, knowing he must banish the smoke. He held, begging his father to intercede; and through the smoke he saw the flame again, brilliant yellow, true gold.

We are this, you fool! he cried down at his maniacal brother, the tormented angel.

The flame increased, engulfing them both, more powerful than acid to melt their enmity, its magnetism greater than the giant magnet of the graveyard; the flame lifted Superman and Kent together, and because it was older, the flame melded them together through knowledge, the dancing light. Kent felt himself merge with the black-robed angel, felt their paradoxical opposition fade.

Superman, held in his arms, vanished with all his blackness into Kent's body. Kent felt the antagonism of the force diminishing, felt it become a ghost within him; he lay alone in the dust of the graveyard, victor over himself.

He rose slowly, in the wreckage of the place, and looked around. Its ugliness seemed now like a grim sort of beauty, and the gray smoke a sacred veil. It blew over him, and away. He opened his shirt. Upon his chest was the true S, in red and gold. A moment later he stood in the complete uniform of his higher calling, its colors restored, his cape brilliant once more.

"A senseless battle," he said to himself, and vowed that it must never happen again; even an immortal can spend his gift if he isn't careful.

He leapt into the sky, and turned overhead, in the direction of the North Atlantic.

"Oh no," said the first mate on the listing tanker, "here he comes again."

The crew of the tanker watched in fear as

Superman circled in the sky. "He's gettin' set to dump us . . ."

Superman surveyed the extent of the oil spill, a great lake floating on the waves below. With breath like the wind god, Superman blew the spilled oil in a stream toward the gaping hull of the boat. The oil poured back in, gallon after gallon, until the sea was clean.

"Horray, horray!" The deck was filled with shouting, as the merchant seamen saw—the Man of Steel had come to his senses again, was no longer a speeding torpedo trying to sink them in the lowlands, but a friend, that mysterious one all sailors see sometime or other, be it the dolphin or the god astride him. They watched as Superman rode upon the waves, his heat-vision radiating out to the hull and repairing its halves, as the halves of his own nature had been repaired.

"My god," said the captain, staring down at the most incredible welding job he'd ever seen at sea.

"Sorry for the trouble, sir," said Superman, flashing by him, and then vanishing, over the horizon.

17

Gus Gorman's computer was four stories high. Occupying an enormous cave at one end of the Grand Canyon, it was industrial giantism in motion, a machine as big as a building, and speaking a resounding language of beeps and blips that echoed down in the ravine.

Pylons and power lines soared above it, and decks and ledges protruded from it, reached by moving elevators and ladders, and it ran all by itself. This was Gus's vision realized—a computer as big as the high school he'd been thrown out of. He believed he had now shown them what was what.

"Yessir," he said, looking down from the rim

of the canyon toward the cave, "that's some machine."

He was holding the reins of a donkey, with whom he was preparing to descend along a canyon path, to inspect his creation.

Standing beside him were Ross and Vera Webster, and Loreli Ambrosia. They would not be descending by donkey, but by hot-air balloons mounted on bicycle seats, which would lower them into the canyon.

"This is fun," said Loreli, whose balloon was a shocking pink.

"Fun?" said Ross Webster. "The fun's just starting. Wait till Superman finds us, then you'll see fun."

Gus stepped forward, twirling his donkey reins. "You *want* to mess with Superman?"

"Can't wait, pal," said Ross. "I even left him a little message back at the penthouse, in case he stops there first."

"Let's go," said Vera, impatiently. "I want to be ready for him when he falls into our trap." She climbed onto her bicycle seat and prepared to launch. Irritably, she turned toward Gus. "I don't see why you can't balloon down like the rest of us."

Gus stepped back with his donkey. "I ain't about to mess with no balloon-bike. You folks go right ahead, I'll catch you 'bout a half-hour from now." Saying so, he started to lead his donkey down the canyon path.

He was a small figure in the immense landscape—

just a young man from the streets who'd sought to improve himself, and in the process lost his way. Now he led a donkey down a canyon trail toward the largest computer ever built, and what had it gained him?

"...'bout one thousand shares preferred stock, an' a solid-gold yo-yo. I ain't been doin' too bad." He talked to the donkey as they descended, and then watched as Ross and Vera Webster, followed by Loreli, launched their vehicles from the canyon heights.

They floated down by him on their balloon-bikes, waving.

Gus shook his head. That Loreli was some pink balloon herself. "...be right down, Lor'li, don't go pressin' any buttons without me..."

Gus watched as the balloon-bikes sank out of sight, into the depths of the canyon. Riding a balloon was not in his program; soon he'd have his own executive jet to fly him around until the gas shortage let up. Couple of sharp pilots and his own Psychic Nutritionis' to bring him champagne and arrange his pillow.

"...fly down to Tia Juana for the weekend..." He patted the donkey's neck. "You ever been there, brother? Got some hot-lookin' mules make you feel a whole lot better..."

The donkey nodded, bridle swaying, saddle creaking. Gus talked on, down the long trail at day's end, which was closer than he knew...

Below, the balloon-bikes were landing, at the entrance to the great cave. Loreli and the Websters dismounted from their bicycle seats and entered the dark cave.

"Where's the light switch?" asked Loreli.

"Where do you usually find a light switch?" answered Vera sharply. She was angry that Ross had brought this dumb slut along, but he'd insisted he needed a leg massage every four hours.

The light came on, and the computer stood visible before them, beeping, talking to itself, running through its gigantic program.

"Wow," said Loreli, "what a jukebox."

Ross Webster gestured modestly, both arms outstretched: "The Ultimate Computer! I created it! I've done it again. I've trumped the world." The great humanitarian radiated joy; he hadn't been this happy since he'd sold rotten rice in a famine.

"Come on," said Vera, eagerly. "Let's give it a dry run."

"We've got to wait until Gus gets here, Sis," said Ross Webster. "That halfwit's the only one who can run it."

Vera Webster drew herself up proudly. "Like fish he is. I know enough about computers to put a Phd to shame."

"Vera, you?" asked Webster, deeply puzzled. Throughout their childhood, Vera had shown little aptitude for electronics, other than as a living transformer whose toenails glowed when he plugged her into house current. Often enough he'd wanted to put a light bulb in her mouth and take her on the *Ed Sullivan Show,* but she'd refused. Could this be the same Vera, walking toward the computer control panel?

Gripping a ladder that led to it, she began to climb. "You didn't think I was going to let that yo-yo run our show, did you?"

Ross Webster followed her, immensely impressed at her confidence. His only regret was that he *hadn't* put a light bulb in her mouth, long ago, or turned her into a tube of human fluorescence, which was project number 29 in the early kits. "Sis, this is wonderful," he said, gripping the ladder. "You truly amaze me."

"I did it for you, Bubba," she said, her voice choked with emotion. At last, she could show him her competence. She climbed off the ladder, onto the deck in front of the central console. The terrace was filled with controls, hundreds of buttons, lighted dials, video display screens. Vera's eyes glowed; it was for this moment she'd stayed up night after night on the horsehair mattress.

She sat in a chair at the center, with access to all the controls. Ross and Loreli came up behind her, even the petulant Loreli impressed by Vera's mastery.

Vera threw a switch and the machine's low hum increased suddenly, to an advanced mode. "Bubba, engage those levers on your right to activate the Alpha Circuits and lock the modular grid."

Ross Webster followed her orders, and the left side of the four-story structure lit up, lights blinking, electrodes crackling, digital dials alive.

"You!" Vera snapped at Loreli. "Activate circuits twenty-nine through W-seven and start Full Power Coordinates on Exterior Defensive Systems!"

"In other words," said Loreli, regaining her poise, "push this red button."

She did so, and the right side of the Ultimate Computer lit up. At the same time an electronic alarm sounded, echoing throughout the cave. Ross Webster swung around.

"He's here!"

"Oh, Superman," squealed Loreli, remembering the night of nights Superman had spent with her in the penthouse, when he was crazed with desire and madly delightful; she couldn't know that it was only the shadow of greatness she'd tumbled with in the firelight, that the real Superman was someone else entirely. So she was confident now that she could wrap him around her finger. "... oh, Superman, where are you? It's me, Loreli, up here..."

"Cut the mush, you tramp," said Vera angrily, for she knew Superman had not come to pay a social call. "He's after our skin."

"He can have mine, anytime," said Loreli, purring in her kittenish way, and arranging her skirt, just a little higher over her knees.

Vera snorted in disgust, for sex with Superman or any man was not in her program; all business, she led her brother to a covered panel. "Enjoy yourself, Bubba," she said, and flipped it open, revealing a large video screen, complete with joysticks. Entering the screen from above was a tiny computerized figure of Superman, whose image indicated he was sailing closer to them in the canyon.

Vera Webster joined her brother at the controls, pressing buttons marked Exterior Defense.

"Let the game begin," said Ross Webster, excitedly.

Vera pressed another button and a panel board lit up.

MISSILE READY

A low rumbling sound filled the control room as, from beneath the canyon floor, sliding panels opened, revealing a rocket launchpad. The launchpad slowly rose, into position, protecting the entry to the canyon.

Upon Ross Webster's video screen, the tiny image of Superman grew larger. And ranged below it were the images of the missiles about to be deployed. "Fire!" cried Ross delightedly, and the missiles flew across the screen.

Out in the canyon, the Man of Steel was greeted by the sudden volley, which struck him directly and blasted him up the canyon; Ross Webster's video lit up with a score of 13,000.

"I got him!" shouted Webster. "I shot down the Super Sap!"

Vera smiled at her brother. They hadn't played like this in years . . .

But outside, picking himself up off the canyon floor, was an angry Superman. Stopping a speeding bullet was one thing, but being hit in the chest by a salvo of missiles was quite another; very well, if they were going to play tough, so would he.

Witness to this display of firepower was Gus Gorman, at the foot of the trail with his donkey. "...rockets flyin' every which way...somebody liable to get hurt. Could be *me*..."

Superman's speeding form sailed by him, into the cave, and Gus hurried in after him, hoping to act as mediator, a role he believed himself masterful in, another delusion, of course.

Ahead, speeding through the cave, Superman found his way to the control deck of the computer, and landed amidst his foes. "Alright, Webster, pack it in."

"Hi, honey," said Loreli, striking a provocative pose.

"I don't know you, lady," said Superman.

"But the other night—" protested the foolish girl.

"That wasn't me," said Superman. "That guy's gone." He turned to Webster. "And you're next."

Vera, hysteric that she was, shrieked in her chair and swiveled back to the control panel. "Don't you threaten my Bubba!"

She punched another button, and a tremendous zap of blue-and-white electrical energy shot out of the computer and jolted Superman to the ground.

These people, thought Superman, are trying my patience.

Ross Webster chuckled. "Welcome to the wonderful world of computers, Superman. How do you like my machine?''

Superman held his temper, in order to teach with wisdom rather than with violence. He pointed at the machine. "Typical of your kind, Webster. Instead of using it to help others, all the four of you want is to help yourselves.''

Gus Gorman, who'd just climbed up onto the deck, drew back at being included in the group. "Four of us? Not me, man.''

"That's only his *last* name,'' said Loreli. "He likes to be called *Super*man.'' Still intent on ingratiating herself with Superman, she swiveled closer to him, but Gus intervened.

"Hey, I'm not with them!''

"You could have fooled me,'' said Superman, staring Gus down, with eyes that made poor Gus ashamed for all the trouble his weird gift had caused. If only Superman had come along in my formative years, thought Gus, I wouldn't be in this jam today. But no, I was out shootin' dice, gettin' wasted, layin' down some bad habits which have culminated in buildin' the biggest goddamn computer the world ever saw, one you could not hide if you wanted to. "Ok, Superman, I seen the light. Let's pull the plug on this sucker—''

He moved forward, with Superman, but Vera had rotated toward the control board again, and once more was feverishly pressing buttons. "We've got something for *you*, Superman!'' she cried, hysterical repression sounding in every syllable.

An invisible wave field passed out of the machine, and Superman crashed into it with a loud thunk; the substance then wrapped itself around him, encasing him in a thick bubble. Colored gases began to churn inside it, as the temperature in the bubble shot madly upward. "We've got you now, you big stupid goon!" shouted Vera.

"Give it to him, Sis," said Ross Webster, and Vera pressed another button. The capsule lifted, and spun around the vast interior, preparing to project Superman to the ocean and dump him there, forever.

His radiant eyes burned with power, a sliver of the sun of Krypton flaming in them, and the capsule's molecular structure collapsed.

Ross Webster's jaw fell open, as he realized for the first time that he had chosen to play with the wrong adversary. But the great humanitarian leader kept calm, showing his courage under fire. "He's coming!" he screamed, hiding behind his sister. "He's going to get me!"

"Don't bet on it," said Vera, and played her filthiest card. Her blunt fingertip punched another button, and from the center of the machine a green ray emanated.

"That's Kryptonite!" shouted Gus. "No!"

"Yes!" shrieked Vera. "This time we *got it right!*"

Ross Webster's voice rose above his sister's, as he turned to Gus. "It's your genius, pal! You built the machine that can find anybody's weak spot. You're going to go down in history as the man who killed Superman!"

The green ray struck and Superman fell, profound weakness filling his limbs.

... they've beaten me ...

The devastating beam attacked every pore of his superhuman form. He was caught in a suffocating cloud of green, his death-color, his doom.

Gus Gorman raced to the edge of the deck, whipped out his executive yo-yo, tossed it over a guy wire, and launched himself.

Gripping both ends of the yo-yo string, he sailed down the guy wire and landed on the floor below, in the Generator Area.

... talkin' 'bout dismantlin' this pile of junk, and save Superman's ass ...

Every niche of the monstrosity known to him, he tracked quickly to the heart. From his pocket he whipped out a tiny screwdriver and undid just one screw coupling. The machine shut down, instantly, its power source gone.

"You traitor!" shouted Ross Webster from above. He scrambled down the ladder and raced into the Generator Area, where Gus stood, the single screw in his fingers. "Put it back in!" shouted Webster.

"Puttin' it where it won't do no harm," said Gus, and popped it in his mouth. A moment later, it was lodged in his throat, sideways.

... good god a'mighty, thought Gus, eyes bulging out as he frantically tried to swallow the screw.

This is what I get for all my *bull*-shit ...

... screw stuck in my goddamn windpipe ...

... an' Ross Webster jumpin' on me.

"Spit it out!" Webster was trying to pry Gus's

mouth open, and knocked him to the floor, where by coincidence one of the workmen had left a Twinkie wrapper and half a can of stale root beer. Gus grabbed it, and swallowed.

Go, baby, go . . . go all the way down . . .

He pleaded as he'd never pleaded before, not even with fancy ladies.

. . . go . . . all the way . . .

Ross Webster, enraged, grabbed Gus from behind and applied a violent Heimlich Maneuver. But the screw was down and Gus, glad to be alive, socked Ross in the jaw. The humanitarian sagged, into a heap.

"Been wantin' to do that for some time," said Gus, dusting off his alligator pants, and stepping over the fallen Webster.

On the control deck above, Superman was slowly climbing to his feet, the effects of the Kryptonite neutralized. He held to the guardrail and nodded down to Gus. "Thanks for—"

An unearthly roar filled the cave, as the machine came to life again, glowing hotter and brighter than it had before, its enormous frame crackling with energy.

Loreli, who'd had quite enough excitement now to last her a lifetime, turned to Vera. "Make it stop!"

Vera, at the control board, was frantically pushing buttons. "I can't! It's out of control!"

"But how? Where is it getting the power from?"

Vera looked above her, at the wild energy probes leaping from the head of the machine—lightninglike bursts that went through the ceiling of the cave. The probes, out in the open air, darted up the pylons and power lines. Gus's hideous creation was feeding itself, from the source . . .

The power lines glowed red from the energy demand, and suddenly across the state and the nation, all power was drained toward one instrument— the Ultimate Computer.

TV sets went off, causing mass hysteria and withdrawal psychosis. Factories stopped, hospitals were struck:

"Alright, Nurse, I'm inside the brain now. If I make a single slip this man will be a babbling idiot for the rest of his life—''

"Doctor, oh my god, the lights—''

The lights were out, everywhere, except in the Computer. It glowed in its cave once more, and the deadly green Kryptonite shot forth again, hitting Superman full force.

Weakened by the first exposure, the Man of Steel was vulnerable, and twisted like a rag doll as the ray struck. He sank, in a sea of nightmare green.

Gus, watching from below, was horrified. He did not want to go down in history as the man who killed Superman, as his family would be disgraced and the jail sentence would be extreme.

. . . be washin' the warden's socks for two hundred years . . .

He grabbed a fire ax and raced up to the deck. A tortured expression crossed his face as he struck at the mechanism, for this was his electronic dream he was destroying. But it was considerably better than viewing life through an electrified fence in the Colorado Penal System.

...bustin' you all up, babe, beatin' your brains in...

Chunks of glass and steel fell to the floor. The Kryptonic ray blacked out, but the machine retaliated against its creator. A beam of energy shot out and lifted Gus into the air.

"...hey, brother, put me down! Hey, I *made* you. I'm the one who gave you your..."

Throwin' me through the air, directly toward the wall...

...hittin' the wall full force...

...slidin' down it, every bone in my body busted...

...fallin' on the floor in a heap over here in the corner...

Gus slowly passed out, but Superman had gotten to his feet, his strength returning. Loreli, terrified of the Computer's mad violence, raced toward him. "Save us, Superman! Get us out of here!"

To some she might have appeared fetching. To Superman she was a blur, of no consequence. He turned, and streaked from the cave, into the sky.

"Superman!" cried Loreli. "Don't leave us alone in here! Superman—"

The helpless girl, so accustomed to having things her own way, looked around in terror as the Computer shook with electronic cascades of power. For a moment, she was paralyzed. Her life passed before her, and she remembered she had only six credits to go for a doctorate in philosophy. Somehow this gave her a burst of strength from deep within, and she raced toward the ladder.

"Get out of my way, you tramp!" Vera Webster was right behind, trying to save herself too.

But she'd pressed one button too many in her earlier glee.

A panel opened now, and poor Vera was sucked back across the deck and drawn into the Computer, her body crashing against a section of its circuitry.

"...Ross...help...Ross..."

A monstrous transformation began to take place, one prefigured in Vera's childhood long ago, when her brother had wired her for sound. She was suddenly part of the gigantic grid of the Computer. Circuitry appeared beneath her skin. Her face was distorted into a grotesque inhuman cubistic form. Charges of electricity passed through her body, lighting it up. An unearthly sound came from her throat.

Her arm crackled, and a silvery sphere of magnetic energy shot out; Loreli was caught by it as she fled across a terraced grid. Her motion was stopped and she was lifted into the air.

"...no...no..."

The magnet swung her to the wall of the cave, and pinned her there, kicking and screaming. Her shoes fell off and her hairdo was almost ruined; she saw the error of her ways, that she should have sold her Webcoe shares after they'd split, and then split herself, to Palm Springs.

Vera, meanwhile, had grown still more dehumanized, her body glowing like a Forty-second Street marquee. She had become a living tube of fluorescence.

A hideous yellow probe shot from her forehead, sending a ray of searing intensity across the room. Perhaps Vera was taking revenge on her brother for having tormented her in childhood; now, as he regained consciousness and struggled to his feet, the yellow beam stopped him in his tracks, burning off his eyebrows and bowtie. He tried to move, but he was held fast in the yellow beam like someone encased in a quarter-pound of margarine. His life passed before him, and he saw the error of his ways; he should have electrocuted his sister at an early age, for look what she'd become, fire shooting out her nose, lights coming from her head—a monster who held him in a fiendish grip.

"Vera," he groaned, "let me go . . . I'll give you the Company . . . you can have . . . my Krugerrands . . ."

But Vera was beyond his voice, caught in the machine's electronic embrace. A grotesque smile seemed to have crossed her face, as 220 billion pulsations per second passed through her, vibrating her organs. A lonely woman, possibly she mistook this electronic caress for love, her teeth lighting up, her hair curling.

Loreli, magnetized to the wall, kicked her pretty legs and screamed. " . . . Superman . . . Superman, help me! Didn't our night together mean *anything* to you?"

Possibly it did. But Superman would never admit it, and in any case the Man of Steel was nowhere near. His streaking form was passing over Chanooga Lake, and descending toward the chemical plant he'd saved a month ago.

The receptionist looked up, astonished, as the Man of Steel entered the lobby. "S . . . S . . . Superman?"

"I must see your senior chemist, at once."

Superman was escorted by a grateful staff into the laboratory of the company's mad scientist who, deeply engrossed in a study of bread mold growing on his own thumb, hardly noticed the Man of Steel behind him.

"Sir," said Superman, "I need your help."

"Is that so? Well, what about this?" The mad scientist showed his furry thumb to Superman.

Twin rays of light shot from Superman's eyes, burning off the mold. A hideous smell, like that of a burning mackintosh, momentarily filled the lab. "Thank you," said the mad scientist, coolly. "In another hour, my entire body would have been moldy."

"I need some of that Beltric acid," said Superman.

"Concentrated Number eight? It's yours." The mad scientist whipped a cannister of it from his shelf and handed it to Superman.

The Man of Steel put it beneath his cape, bowed graciously, and streaked from the building, back into the sky.

The country passed below him, wilderness and farm, the landscape a blur to his racing eyes. He was himself again, working for humanity, its guardian angel and friend; he'd lost his grip awhile back and played the drunken fool; a vile interlude, but at least he now knew he was not the goody-good everyone thought he was. He too cast a shadow, deeper than most, a shadow filled with cruel intent. He must live with this knowledge, and show mercy when human selfishness came his way.

Except for Ross Webster. Him I put out of business.

Into the Grand Canyon he sailed, dropping to the cave mouth once again, and entering, with the cannister of acid hidden beneath his cape.

On entering the cave, he saw Ross Webster suffocating in the yellow ray. At once, Superman stepped in front of the ray, absorbing it and freeing Webster. The humanitarian crawled feebly out of its range, flopping like a fried egg.

Seeing his adversary helpless, Superman turned back toward the Ultimate Computer. It answered his gaze with a pair of giant arms that came out like pinball flippers—a vestige of the countless hours Gus Gorman had wasted in his youth, working such flippers in neighborhood dives. Now the giant flippers scooped Superman directly inward, toward the glowing circuitry where Vera Webster was fixed like an old radio tube. The magnetic field gripped him and drew him into the bowels of the machine.

Cobwebs of electricity formed around him, seeking to distort and dehumanize him. Fighting these fiendish elements, he played his own card—the cannister of acid which he placed at the core of the machine, where the heat was at its most intense.

The acid boiled, bright orange. It popped and jumped from its container, splattering the walls and workings of the inner chamber. The gel–like substance attached itself to the wires, burning them through and melting their contacts. Short circuits flared up everywhere in the machinery.

"...and now, you ugly monster," said Superman, brushing aside the webs of electricity, "...destroy yourself."

Explosions and burn-outs rent the machine, story by story, to its highest level. Loreli dropped from the wall, into a disheveled heap of chic sportswear and torn stockings. Vera fell from the circuitry, her body limp and unconscious, the glow fading from it and her hair uncurling.

Then everything collapsed, as the Great Computer self-destructed, and the once-elegant machine became a pile of rock and rubble.

Vera, Ross, and Loreli found themselves pinned inside a slide of burnt-out panels, wires dangling around them. Ross Webster scratched weakly on the walls, wondering what he'd done to deserve a day like this.

18

The oil fields went back to pumping, and gasoline flowed across America again. Above the great and prosperous nation flew Superman, with a bankrupt Gus Gorman hanging from his fist.

Gus frantically tried to get his legs tucked up around Superman. Superman looked at him. "You're perfectly safe."

"Funny, I don't *feel* safe..." Gus opened one eye, looked down at the desert far below.

I need a magazine, keep my mind from wanderin' to the fact I am danglin' up here like the yo-yo that I am...

He decided light conversation might help. "Say, how'd you kill my machine anyway?"

"I didn't kill it, Gus. It died of acid indigestion."

The man have a sense of humor, thought Gus. Maybe he won't take me to jail. Maybe he'll just set me down in that desert somewhere, give me a chance to fend for myself, starvin' to death and dyin' of thirst with coyotes chewin' off my feet. "Put me in the nearest prison yard, Superman. I know my way around from there."

Superman said nothing, just flew on, and soon the desert was left behind them. Gus thought of trying an oblique approach: "What's going to happen to Ross the Boss and those ladies?"

"That's up to the judge, Gus. It's not your problem anymore."

A mountain range passed below them, and Superman swooped low.

My problem is he gonna leave me on a mountaintop with grizzly bears after my ass. "... should be a local jail roun' here somewhere..." Gus looked over his shoulder. "What do you think 'bout that suggestion?"

Superman's gaze was directed at the horizon far beyond the mountain range, and Gus could only close his eyes again, and pray for the lights of some big city to come up. That was the one wilderness he could survive in, as a kitchen technician.

Washin' dishes, be so nice. Stick my arms in boilin' water, see them come out red as a lobster. Be a good life, go home, have a beer and stare at my big toe. "... hey, hey ... what's goin' on ..."

They were diving toward the hills of West Virginia. A moment later, Gus had the ground beneath his feet again, in the yard of a mining camp.

A pair of miners looked up in amazement from the doorway of their shack, as Superman walked toward a pile of coal. "Can you guys spare a piece of this?"

"Shore, Superman," said one of the miners. "It . . . *is* Superman, ain't it?"

"Hey," said Gus, "who do you think it is? Lookit them red boots . . ." He swaggered in the yard, as if he were Superman's navigator. "This is the Man of Steel, you dig? We been flyin' all goddamn day and we'd like to stretch ourself a bit."

While Gus was stretching, Superman was squeezing the coal in his fist. His great strength compressed the lump of black carbon, which began to glow. What it would normally take centuries to do, he did in seconds, turning the coal into a large glittering diamond.

"Too showy," he said to himself, and squeezed it again, compressing it still further, into a more modest size. "Yes, that'll do just fine." He turned toward the miners. "Does your boss use a computer in this operation?"

"Yeah, a small one. Why?"

"You tell him I said he can do a lot worse than giving Gus Gorman a job." Superman smiled farewell and took off into the air.

Gus craned his neck, watching the red cape flutter, grow smaller, and vanish. "Take it easy,

Superman. You're a fine dude . . . even though you lef' me here in West Virginia . . .''

He turned toward the miners, who had arms like coal shovels and little squinty eyes like cave bats'.

These are some hard-lookin' crackers.

Probably crack *me*.

Carryin' shotguns, no doubt, 'cross the back of the cab in their truck.

Use an individual like myself for target practice in the mornin'.

"Well," said one of the miners, "you got good references. So if y'all want that job—"

"Thing I actually want is the bus station," said Gus.

"That way—about ten miles."

Without hesitation, Gus turned.

. . . track along through the bushes, travel inconspicuously in a ditch, slide into town under cover of darkness, and then buy me a one-way ticket north.

Seem like a good plan.

"Hey," said one of the miners. "Y'all really fly with Superman?"

Gus turned around. "Hey, Soup and me, we go back a long way. We generally help each other out, you see, like just yesterday we was in this cave?" He paused, and looked around at the desolate landscape.

Best thing be for me to move my ass.

While I still have one . . .

He walked off, into the twilight.

19

The room-service trolley pushed through the door, bringing supper for three. Lana Lang and Ricky helped the waiter, arranging the tables and chair in the hotel room. Outside the hotel window, the lights of Metropolis sparkled, and Lana kept looking toward the sky, for the arrival of their guest.

"Will that be all?" asked the waiter.

"Yes, thank you," said Lana, and the waiter wheeled the trolley out and closed the door. A moment later, a knock came.

"He must have forgotten something," said Ricky Lang, and ran to the door.

"Hi," said Clark Kent.

"Mr. Kent! Guess who's having dinner with us tonight!"

Clark turned apologetically toward Lana. "Actually, that's why I stopped by. Superman is very sorry, he wanted to make it but then he—ran into a problem."

Kent knew that Superman's presence, while a thrill for Ricky, would become problematical for Lana. Even his own presence was going to present something of a problem. He knew that all he could really do for Lana was help her out, get her started in the city, and hope she'd meet someone suitable— and not someone who led a double life and held a secret as old as the stars.

Lana's disappointment was clear. "I guess he misses a lot of dinners."

"Well," said Clark, "if you don't mind settling for me—"

"Any day," said Lana, warmly.

Just keep it simple, said Kent to himself. You've given yourself to everyone on Earth, and no one woman can ever hope to claim you. Though this woman . . . has such soft eyes . . .

He fumbled in his pocket. "Superman asked me to give you something. He and I, we talk all the time, and when he heard about you pawning your diamond, well—he sort of found this lying around and thought you might like to have it."

He gave her the diamond, set in a simple ring. She stared at it for a long time, and when she looked up at him her eyes were moist. She tried to speak, but couldn't, and finally could only throw her arms around Clark.

"Wow!" shouted Ricky. "A ring from Superman! Lemme see, Mom!'' He jumped up, knocking over a dish of candies.

''Here, I'll get those,'' said Clark, glad of a chance to escape Lana's embrace. He knelt on the carpet where the candies were scattered, at Lana's feet.

The door opened and Brad Wilson burst in, having traveled all day with the fantasy of saving Lana Lang from the big city with a proposal of marriage. Instead he found her with a sparkling new diamond on her finger and Clark Kent kneeling before her.

''Why—you sonofa—'' Brad leapt at Kent, fist swinging. His drunken punch went wild, and he staggered past Kent. Turning clumsily, he snarled at the mild-mannered reporter. ''Kent, I hate you. I always hated you. And you know why?'' Wilson's pickled mind struggled to find the appropriate reason, which slowly surfaced like the olive in a martini. ''Because you're *nice*. And nice guys finish—''

He lowered his head and charged, roaring like a buffalo. Clark ducked and Wilson catapulted over him and out the open door, onto the room-service trolley.

His drunken momentum carried him down the hall, spread-eagled on the trolley. The hallway carpet rushed beneath his bloodshot eyes, and it seemed to him he was flying across the goal line once more, into the end zone, to the cheers of the crowd, when actually he was crashing into the open elevator, to the distinct distaste of the elderly couple riding there.

Wilson's head struck the elevator wall, rendering him unconscious on the room-service trolley, a variety of condiments decorating his hair and suit.

The woman looked down in disgust. "No wonder they sent it back."

In the offices of the *Daily Planet*, Perry White was congratulating his star reporter: "Lois, I've got to hand it to you. Who else could manage to turn a three-week tropical vacation into a front-page story that's going to blow the lid off government corruption in the Caribbean..."

Lois smiled coyly. "I knew I was onto something when that taxi driver kidnapped me."

Clark Kent joined in. "You're the best, Lois."

"Well, your high school reunion article was terrific, too, Clark," she said, a sly tone in her voice. "Especially that little bit about the girl back home. Tell you what, I'll take you to lunch and you can tell me more about it."

"Gee, I'm sorry, Lois. But I've already got a lunch date. With Mr. White's new secretary."

"Oh?"

The door to White's office opened, and Lana Lang came in with some papers for White. She laid them on the editor's desk and White stood up, between the two women. "Lois, meet Lana Lang. She's Smallville's latest gift to Metropolis."

Lana put out her hand. "I'm so pleased to meet you, Miss Lane. I like your writing a lot."

"Thanks," said Lois woodenly, staring down at the ring on Lana's finger. "I like your sparkler."

"Me too," said Lana, happily. "I couldn't believe it when Clark gave it to me."

"Clark gave you—?" Lois looked around in confusion, but before an explanation could be given, Miss Henderson opened the office door. "Mr. White, look what I've got for you!" she cried, backing in.

"My god, what is the woman up to now," grumbled White.

"A new machine!" shrieked the birdlike Miss Henderson, wheeling in the new Bingo Jingo apparatus. "It's completely electronic."

White stared moodily at the large plastic dome. He'd just settled out of court with that madwoman who'd broken her neck in South America . . .

"Alright," he said, stepping reluctantly up to the machine. "Where's the handle?"

"There *is* no handle," giggled Miss Henderson, girlishly. "You just push a button."

Someone should push you, Miss Henderson, thought Perry White, as he put his finger on the control. "Now what?"

Plastic balls began to leap within the dome. There was a grinding sound, and smoke curled out from beneath the machine.

"Goodness . . ." Miss Henderson bent over the controls.

"Get that popcorn maker outta here," growled White. The dome exploded and plastic balls flew around the office. " . . . what in the . . ." White threw up his hands, too late, as one sailed into his open mouth.

Clark Kent, watching the machine self-destruct, suddenly remembered: he had some unfinished business.

He backed away from the flying balls. "... excuse me, folks..."

"Kent!" shouted White, believing himself in danger from the berserk Bingo mechanism. Smoke clouded the office, and through it Clark Kent vanished.

His path led him out of the *Planet* offices, and into a favorite telephone booth. Seconds afterward, he was streaking across the sky.

In Pisa, a humble souvenir salesman had recently borrowed from the Mafia in order to lay in a new supply of remodeled plastic Towers of Pisa. He stood before them now, admiring them. Then he turned toward the Tower.

They were *exactly* like it, standing perfectly straight.

"... getta you souvenir Towers ... justa like the real t'ing..." He called to the passing tourists, who turned suddenly, cameras pointed upward.

"Look! There in the sky!"

"It's—"

Superman flew to the top of the Tower and laid his grip of steel upon it. Slowly, he brought the famous landmark back to its familiar leaning angle. "There, that's much better."

"*Cretino! Stronzo!*" The souvenir salesman wept

with rage, fist in the air. He turned, knocked all his perfectly straight Towers over, jumped up and down on them, and punched himself in the head.

"...*mamma mia...whattamy gonna do now...mamma mia...*"

Above in the sky, Superman circled, a warm smile on his face.

The crowd cheered, and Superman saluted. The world was safe in his hands.

He sped away, into the clouds.

SUPER HEROES
from WARNER BOOKS

___**SUPERMAN: LAST SON OF KRYPTON**
by Elliot S. Maggin (U82-319, $2.25)
A tiny space ship leaves the dying planet Krypton, carrying the infant who will become Earth's Superman. Here's the enthralling tale of his childhood in Smallville, his emergence as newsman Clark Kent, his battles with arch-enemy Luthor. It's the one and only original story.

___**SUPERMAN AND SPIDER-MAN**
by Jim Shooter, John Buscema
& Joe Sinott (U91-757, $2.50)
For the first time in paperback form, the two great heroes are united in an incredible adventure—all in terrific color.

___**BATMAN VS. THE INCREDIBLE HULK**
by Len Wein, Jose Garcia Lopez
and Dick Giordano (A30-244, $2.95)
The most explosive confrontation in heroic history between two of the most popular Super Heroes.™

The Starfishers Trilogy

FUN from
WARNER BOOKS